Totally Bound Publishing books by Katherine McIntyre

Tribal Spirits
Forged Alliances
Forged Decisions
Forged Contracts
Forged Futures
Forged Redemption

The Whitfield Files
Of Tinkers and Technomancers

Tribal Spirits

FORGED ALLIANCES

KATHERINE MCINTYRE

Forged Alliances
ISBN # 978-1-913186-13-5

Interior text design by Claire Siemaszkiewicz
Totally Bound Publishing

Published in 2018 by Totally Bound Publishing, United Kingdom.

Totally Bound Publishing is an imprint of Totally Entwined Group Limited.

FORGED ALLIANCES

Dedication

To the female alphas in my life, who are always an inspiration.

Chapter One

Sierra was spoiling for a fight.

She slammed into the Beaver Tavern's door shoulder first, amber light spilling on her, and the scent of tobacco threading through the air when she entered. Wooden planks creaked under her boots from her tread as she quick-stepped to the oaken bar on the opposite side. Three things lit her match without fail—abusive assholes, idiots who didn't use their turn signals and unannounced shifters moving in on her territory.

Inside, her beast snapped at its confines, begging her to shift, to take to the woods and keep running, never turning back. Except leaving wasn't an option, not since she'd become alpha of the Red Rock pack years ago. Sounds of the bar in full swing washed over her, from the shouts and laughs of the regulars to the *clunks* of heavy pint glasses hitting the tables.

"Sierra, what's up your ass?" Jeremiah called over from a table as a lazy smile reached his hazel eyes. Her Red Rock pack filled the whole bar, since humans kept their distance from predominantly shifter areas, and in this part of Pennsylvania few would come strolling in.

She flipped him the middle finger. "Shut it, Streaky," she called back, garnering a couple of laughs from the pack. After Jer had gotten caught buck-ass naked, stumbling out of at least three different tents at the last Fourth of July party, the nickname had stuck. Sierra beelined to where Raven operated the taps, dispensing dew to this loud and crazy lot. Sierra's body brimmed with unspent tension. *Fight, fight, fight* pounded through her, an untamable urge, and her wolf prowled inside her, restless. As alpha, her rank heightened her tether to the beast, already one step away from primal.

"Shot of whiskey," she growled, needing to regain control. Needing the reset before she engaged with her pack. Raven blinked at her, those deep-set eyes warm and welcoming as she reached for the bottle of Jack. Strands of the bartender's thick black hair drifted over her shoulder as she passed the drink over.

"Boss, go for the whole thing," she said with an amused smile. The bottle hit the counter with a thump, reminding Sierra of the massive inventory piling up in the back. The day she'd won the title of alpha, she'd also earned herself ownership of this dive.

"Thanks," she muttered before unscrewing the cap and taking a swig. The amber liquid sloshed around the bottle, burning once the whiskey hit her lips. She soaked in the bliss, in the five-second distraction from the territorial urges pushing her toward an aggression-fueled pissing contest. Her skin prickled, hackles raised from her earlier run—from the note that had turned this day from sunshine-speckled to hellish.

She sucked down another swig, the burn of alcohol spreading through her before she returned the bottle to the counter. One deep breath, then two, and she started to feel normal again. The beast snarled but backed down. Sierra plopped onto one of the worn leather stools and leaned forward, elbows digging into the polished oak counter. Her tank top was glued to her chest and her thick obsidian locks plastered to her cheeks and her neck. The sweltering heat that swept the region wasn't helping her mood in the slightest.

A hand snaked out in front of Sierra to tug the bottle away as the seat beside her creaked.

"Need to go a couple of rounds?" Finn asked, his dark eyes dancing with amusement at her barely contained rage. "Whatever's got your wolf snapping is hitting the rest of us too. I'm assuming a summer squall's brewing." The beta of her pack dominated the stool, tall, with the lithe muscle of an MMA fighter—fitting, since he taught kickboxing classes six days a week. He'd been her sparring partner for years, and even as a teenager, the bastard had played dirty, sand in the eyes and all.

"Storm's ready to touch down," Sierra muttered, slumping onto the counter. When it came to her pack, she made calls without hesitation—every member from the eldest to the littles had complaints, problems to solve or disputes and fights she managed. However, this problem was in a whole different category. "We've got new neighbors, and they're of the pain-in-my-ass variety."

"Neighbors like us?" Finn asked, beckoning Raven. She sauntered over, eyebrow lifted at being summoned that way. He tilted his head toward the taps, and she rolled her eyes before pouring him a pint. Sierra withheld her smirk, entertained by watching big dominant guys like Finn getting sassed back. All those powerful wolves didn't make dating easy though, especially being alpha. As much as the guys liked to talk the talk of handling a woman more dominant than them, few could walk the walk. She swallowed age-old bitterness of the lesson she'd learned the hard way.

Before she could respond to Finn, the door of the bar creaked open, drawing her attention.

She hadn't even turned around before her wolf started yanking at the chain, begging to come out. The scent hit her nose at once, not the familiar one of her Red Rock pack, but this unfamiliar one that brushed her fur the wrong way. Claws pricked out from her nails before she could stop herself, and she wasn't the only one. A low growl emerged beside her as Finn picked up the foreign scent.

"Mislabeled the sign," a cocky voice called from the door. "Should read 'Doggie Daycare' with the number of pups packed into this place." The man's eyes twinkled at his less-than-funny joke, and an amused grin spread on his face. He walked in with a graceful stride, the liquidity of his movements betraying his kind, as if a cat could ever disguise its nature. Chairs squeaked as folks leaped up, teeth bared and claws out as her Red Rocks prepared to rush the intruder. A blonde chick and a long-limbed toothpick of a guy strode in behind him with similar refinement to their movements.

Sierra barely controlled herself as she forced her claws back into place. Out of everyone, she had to rein in her beast because she carried the responsibility of an entire pack on her shoulders. "You'd figure with so many pups under one roof, a kitty cat wouldn't be stupid enough to wander in."

"Oh, you know, curiosity and all that." His white teeth gleamed against his tanned skin. "You folks give the warmest welcomes to newcomers." He tugged on the end of his baseball cap before crossing through the crowded bar without a care. The cocky bastard ignored the bristling wolves on either side begging to leap forward, each lethal in his or her own right. Either he had brass balls or he had lost his common sense a few states back. A couple of members of Sierra's pack glanced her way, begging permission to lunge at the intruder and take him down.

"Well, love notes as charged as yours tend to inspire passionate responses." Sierra forced a grin, baring her teeth in the process. The note had been simple. The Silver Springs pack—a group of mountain-lion shifters with the reputation for being mean motherfuckers—were searching for a new home. Right in the middle of Red Rock territory. Asshole thought he was hilarious, leaving a trail of puppy chew toys strewn through her normal jogging path.

Sierra began her own approach, each step coiled with tension. Not like she would attack him unprovoked, but the moment she caught sign of a claw or fang from these intruders, all bets were off.

Sierra stepped up to the guy, the scent of woodsmoke and fresh earth saturating the air in his proximity. He must've been running through the forest and recently shifted to human. "Welcome to my territory," she said, placing a hand out with emphasis. "I'm Sierra Kanoska, alpha of the Red Rock pack."

The man's eyes widened with interest as he clapped his large, callused palm against hers and shook. Even though he towered at least a foot above her, Sierra thrust her chin up, not intimidated in the slightest. Men tended to rely too heavily on their size instead of realizing one well-placed blow would make them crumble. And Sierra had honed her body into a weapon.

"Dax Williams, alpha of the Silver Spring pack. Pleased to make your acquaintance." The challenge dwelled in his tone of voice, in the openness of his stance and the flare of his nostrils as he soaked in the scent of her surrounding wolves. The smirk on his face was one Sierra's knuckles itched to knock off. The bastard had barely been here five minutes, but already she hated him. He stepped away, sidling past her to rest his forearms on the bar. "Don't suppose I can get a drink around here?"

Raven glanced over to her, her eyes glowing silver with the same aggression as the rest of them. Sierra slid back onto her stool, giving Raven a nod in return. Until they established why Dax and his cronies had picked her territory to torment and whether they could be convinced to turn away without bloodshed, a pint would be the best way to defuse the powder keg this room had turned into.

"Sorry, we're fresh out of milk," Sierra said with a too-sweet smile.

Dax's lips curled with a wicked smirk. "Pity. Guess I'll have to settle for a pint, then."

The woman behind him took one of the empty stools, her ponytail bouncing as she sat. "Make that three. All our running made Kyle and me thirsty."

Raven stared stony-faced at the counter as she filled Sierra a pint first, then followed with drinks for the intruders, her claws pricking out in the process. The air thickened, and every eye homed in on the three intruders lining the bar by Sierra. She hadn't taken her gaze off them for a second, waiting for a slip-up. The day she'd become alpha she'd swallowed her responsibility pills, but she wasn't a saint.

Dax lifted the closest pint to his lips and his cronies took theirs. Not to be outdone, Sierra tipped hers back, chugging the liquid in an attempt to distract herself from ramming a punch into the too-calm kitty alpha's face. The ale coursed down her throat until foam dripped to her lips, and she slammed the glass on the bar, heat flushing through her at her triumph. The three mountain cat shifters stared at her, sipping at their drinks as if they didn't have a care in the world.

"Pint's over. Since you came rolling up to what's obviously one of our bars, I'm assuming you're ready to discuss business now," Sierra said, leaning forward to place her forearms on the bar. Her braid shifted down her back with the way she thrust her chin forward. "Right now, you're considered guests in our territory. However, if you're here to try and stake a claim, you'll find yourself out on your ass before you can blink."

A couple of growls reverberated around her, including from Finn, who hunched forward, his eyes glowing amber.

"I'd like to see you try." Dax's lips curled into a smile, smug enough to make her say to hell with the consequences and tear into him. He shifted on the seat, near dwarfing it with a lethal, coiled body that spelled dangerous. Despite his calm, the way his blue eyes flashed promised trouble. She'd heard rumors in the breeze of unrest in the Silver Springs region, of the old alpha passing. If these cats had encroached on her territory, they must've arrived for a damn good reason, since he didn't seem the sort to go running from a challenge.

Sierra wasn't alpha just because she'd wiped the floor with the big guys in the pack—hell, most of the strong ones could go toe-to-toe with her. She'd become alpha because she paid attention, she listened and, most importantly, she understood the big picture.

Her brow lifted as she soaked Dax in. *Proud shifter like him wouldn't come slinking in asking for help.* No, he'd bluster on in and start a ruckus, distract, maybe carve out a niche for himself and his cats. Bringing her suspicions up in front of his pack wouldn't help, either, because he had to keep a bold front. She had to figure out a way to get him alone, so they could hash this out alpha-to-alpha.

"Right, keep talking big while you've got your posse at your back," Sierra challenged, pushing him.

He snorted into his pint. "Says the woman with an entire bar full of wolves to hide behind."

"Fine," Sierra responded, hiding her amusement at how fast she'd maneuvered him. "Then let's have this conversation somewhere private. That is, if you aren't too scared." She threw the barb in for good measure but didn't have to fake the heat of challenge in her voice.

Dax's grin widened, revealing teeth as he leaned against the bar. "Darling, if you wanted me somewhere private, all you had to do was ask," he drawled. The languid way he carried himself oozed sensuality and the confidence of a guy who got his way often. Just the sort she'd run roughshod over. Sierra didn't blink, crossing her arms.

Finn tapped her shoulder. "Boss, you don't have to give him the time of day, let alone engage in any one-on-one negotiations. Cats aren't trustworthy."

"My beta's bringing up some pretty good points," she said to Dax in return, getting up from her barstool. "Think you can survive a talk with me without resorting to petty tricks?"

The beanpole, Kyle, jumped in. "And why should we trust you to not launch an ambush once you get him alone?"

Sierra's gaze flashed, her claws pricking out. "Because Red Rocks keep their word." Her voice turned molten and harsh despite the complete control she'd regained. Intimidation against a bitty cat like him came as natural as running water. "Because we don't go intruding on other folks' territories, making demands. We learned a thing or two about honor and loyalty along the way and about defending our home with our lives."

"I believe you," Dax replied. His eyes danced with amusement, blue like the shifting seas. He slid his emptied pint glass across the slick surface of the bar and hopped off his seat. "So why waste any more time?" With his powerful stride, he was halfway across the room in seconds before he turned around to glance at her.

Sierra clenched her jaw. Even though she'd been able to unseat him for a couple of seconds, every interaction with him was a push-pull for power, one seeping beneath her skin like an itch she couldn't scratch. She cast a glance to Finn. "Treat them like guests while they're here," she murmured. "However, if they get aggressive, don't hesitate to slit their throats."

"Please, my pack is nothing but well-behaved," Dax called across the room. "Just tell your puppies to play nice."

Sierra shot Finn one last glance before striding across the room to catch up with Dax. She didn't trust the bastard for a heartbeat. Even though she could hold her own in a fight, the mischief blazing in his eyes and the slick calm he oozed set her nerves on edge. Whatever reason he had for bringing his pack into her territory, one fact remained undeniably true: The man was pure trouble.

Chapter Two

Dax wasn't sure what game the Red Rock alpha played, but she'd piqued his curiosity. He and his packmates had taken a massive risk strolling into the bar since they were intruding on another pack's territory, but he'd always been one for a challenge. Besides, desperate times called for desperate measures. Sierra Kanoska didn't need to know his reasons for arriving in her region and stirring up shit. At least, not yet.

He sauntered after her, stepping out into the humid night. "Hope you're not taking me to some remote location to bury my body in a ditch."

"Like I'd waste the time," Sierra scoffed, tossing her thick braid back. One look at her confirmed who led this pack. Her hips swung back and forth as she walked forward, wearing jeans that highlighted her muscular thighs and the shapely ass Dax couldn't help but admire. Even though he'd received nothing but glares and scowls from the woman, between her clever brown eyes, high cheekbones and pert mouth, she had the sort of looks to turn heads.

"You up for a run?" she asked, her gaze focusing on the fringe of trees past the parking lot situated in front of darkened woods. At the mention of a run, the cat paced inside him, begging to come out and play. Despite Sierra's poor luck in being born a wolf, the charge between them had him intrigued, and she promised to be an interesting playmate.

Dax arched a brow. "I just met you and you're already trying to get me naked?" Goading her while he was a guest in her territory didn't top the Best Idea Chart, but he couldn't help the adrenaline surge every time he provoked a response. Already the predatory side of him pounded a primal beat of claim, dominate and destroy, but he kept himself collared – most of the time.

Sierra scowled, her claws pricking out. "You wish. Where we're heading, there are plenty of spare clothes for the pack to slip into. Try to catch up," she said, her dark eyes flashing with a ferocity that heated his blood. She stripped down with liquid quickness, tossing her crumpled clothes in the grass. Faster than his eyes could follow, she shot forward, jogging to the woods. Fur emerged on her arms, her claws came out and her eyes glowed amber as her body shifted with the fluidity of familiarity. Dax ditched his pants and shirt before bolting to keep up. The cat was barely collared as he got closer and closer to the looming oaks.

The shift overtook him as it always did. Bones stretched to form the muzzle, fur pricked through his skin to coat his body and his field of vision sharpened as he lowered to the ground. The change happened as suddenly as tipping water and as effortlessly as a coursing stream, a transition he exulted in every time. His senses sparked to life, enhanced in this form as the thick leaves on the trees turned a vibrant green and the ground beneath his padded feet grew soft and loamy. The trills of the cicadas in the forest became sweeter and clearer, as all of night's summertime symphony did. Breezes ruffled his fur as he surged through this tangled maze of oaks, pines, and underbrush with reckless abandon, indulging in the soaring joy of the run.

Sierra led the way in the form of a sleek, silver-furred wolf, streaks of black as rich as her hair woven throughout. She raced through the woods with a silence and skill testament not only to her status as alpha, but also the innate familiarity she had of these wilds. He had the same familiarity with his home, the forests he'd learned inside and out during his youth, but for him, returning wasn't an option.

His muscles burned with exertion as he sprinted along, his padded feet pounding the soft earth beneath them. Humidity painted the summer air, threaded with the delicate fragrance of wisteria dangling from a few of the trees.

Every time he reached a casual stride, Sierra would swerve past a massive tree or leap over a wiry shrub, snapping him to attention. If she followed her whip-smart reputation, she'd be testing him the entire way. He'd brought his pack wandering into Red Rock territory for that precise quality, the ruthless intelligence Sierra was known for. After the hellish couple of months Dax had had, he could use more than a little help in that department.

Sierra leaped over a couple of large rocks, bounding with ease. Her amber eyes glinted with the fierceness of her kind, and she ran with a balanced, lupine elegance. Too bad hers paled in comparison to a cat's. He pushed himself to surge ahead, his breaths burning and his muscles working at machine precision until he ran neck and neck with her. Given his precarious position here, he had to establish his strength first.

She veered a sudden right and skidded to a halt so fast his paws churned into the earth, sending stray clippings flying. Only his quicker-than-average reflexes kept him from smashing into a shoddy fence made from a pile of loose stones. The Red Rock alpha hopped over the rocks and padded down the slope to a small cabin constructed of a gorgeous heartwood set in strong lines. The scent of lumber, pine and spent charcoal filtered through the air, tickling his nose.

His claws sank deep into the ground at the distinctive stench of wet wolf marking this place, deep in the heart of Red Rock territory. Sierra loped to the front of the cabin, and, in the blink of an eye, she shifted, standing on two feet in front of the door, utterly nude.

The sight of her punched him in the gut. Nudity was such a common occurrence among shifters that he rarely batted an eye, despite the fair share of athletic, stunning women in his pack. However, even with his intimate familiarity with the female form, he couldn't tug his gaze away from Sierra Kanoska. The woman's Native American blood had given her the sort of raven hair that glowed with mahogany notes in the light. Her bronzed skin deepened several shades at the hollow of her throat, the curve of her ample breasts and the slope of her sinful hips.

She fiddled with the doorknob. Desire pounded a pulse in him as he began shifting into his human form. His fur disappeared, the bristles transformed into his sun-kissed skin and he rose from his crouch to follow her inside the rancher. It wasn't simply her athletic form or the pert ass he could follow for days—Sierra radiated a lethality and wildness he found intriguing, as well as a strength he couldn't help but respect. Not like he'd clue her in on that one.

Dax sauntered into the house past her, his bare feet pressing against the oak floors as the lazy snick-snick of an overhead fan sent a faint breeze through the room. He didn't miss the way her gaze heated when he strolled by, how her stare trailed up and down the length of his body. Her hand rested on her hip, and if she didn't stop eyeing him like a haunch of meat, he wouldn't be able to restrain the blood from flowing southward.

"See something you like?" He glanced back, baring his teeth with a wide grin.

"Nothing worth writing home about," she responded in a dulcet tone and with a smile shades too sweet. She crossed the rancher's open floor, heading for a massive mahogany trunk in the living room. The whole way, she swayed her hips while she walked.

Goddamn tease.

Sierra dipped to reach the trunk, her ass lifted high in the air, so firm he could take a bite out of it. His claws pricked out from his nails, his chest thumping with a punch-two-three beat he couldn't explain for the life of him. He'd need to go hard and fast with one of the pack girls tonight to burn this adrenaline—either that or knock some teeth out with whoever would spar with him. A rolled-up ball of clothes sailed toward him faster than he could blink. He grabbed the bundle before unrolling a flannel tee and black sweats, big enough to fit him.

Dax lifted a brow as he scanned the spare clothes that reeked of wolf. Sierra made quick work of tugging a pair of yoga pants on followed by a racerback tank top, to his dismay.

She glanced over, her full lips pursed with her frown. "They're clothing, genius. Us civilized folk like to wear them while we converse with one another."

He leaned to his right side, his heavy cock brushing against his leg. Her eyes darted his way with a flash of amber, causing his smile to widen. "Pity for you I'm not civilized," he responded, his voice heating up.

Sierra placed both hands on her hips with her chin thrust forward and her arched nose tilted up in defiance. "Put the damn clothes on," she commanded.

"Don't know, I'm feeling a bit overheated," he said, fanning himself. "Delicate constitution and all." Her hands balled into fists, the annoyance fueling his enjoyment. She brimmed with unspent tension begging to be released, and he'd be the first to admit he wouldn't mind tangling with the exquisite woman. Distractions were his specialty, and with the troubles brewing in his sector, he needed one more than ever.

Sierra unleashed a sigh, even though she glanced his way more than a couple of times, her dark eyes glittering. "Fine. If you're going to be a stubborn ass, then we can have this conversation now."

Damn. He'd meant to tease her, but she was obstinate enough to play his power games right back. Looked like he'd be doing this meeting naked. Dax forced a grin and dropped his clothes into a messy pile on the floor. Sierra's nose scrunched in irritation, but she wandered over to one of the three cherrywood chairs with starched mauve fabric over the cushions and sat.

"Care to join me?" she asked, gesturing to one of the other chairs. The scratchy fabric would be a joy for his bare ass. Her eyes twinkled with amusement, and he debated the merits of holding on to his previous statement. Pride won out in the end.

"I like to lean," he responded, walking to the nearby wall and finding a perch against the plaster. "So, what matter was so private we couldn't discuss it back in the bar?" He still hadn't figured out her angle, even though he hadn't ruled out premeditated murder. Out here was a perfect place to dispose of his body after she sliced his throat open.

She lifted a brow. "Why don't you tell me? I've been hearing rumblings about the Silver Springs pack. In the Red Rocks' past dealings with the old alpha, you lot were proud as hell of your space. You wouldn't go slinking to try to claim ours unless you had a problem."

Dax crossed his arms, the cool white wall pressed against his skin, still sticky from the run. He'd been right to come here—Sierra Kanoska lived up to her reputation for being whip smart and tough. Hell, he'd rehearsed this pitch a thousand times in his head on his way to Beaver Tavern, but after meeting her, he knew no used-car-salesman tactics would work. He also couldn't charm her into acquiescence, evident due to her iron control while he participated in this meeting without a stitch on.

He fixed his gaze on her as the gravity of the situation gripped him by the throat. No more escaping, not now. The old anger snapped through him like a struck match as he let out a harsh breath.

"My pack and I are searching for new territory because of an internal conflict," he said. Even admitting their position out loud sliced into his heart like a shard. "My father passed a couple of months back, which left the alpha spot vacant."

Sierra's brows drew together as she hunched forward, giving her full attention. "Sorry about your pops."

Dax shrugged. The bitter thump in his chest served as a clear reminder of his convoluted relationship with his father. They'd never had the camaraderie his older brother and his father shared. If anything, his father had considered him a fuck-up his entire life. Too bad for them he refused to sit around and watch their pack continue his father's bullying tactics, the ones that had cost Silver Springs their reputation years ago.

"Nothing to be sorry about," he responded, wishing the scab didn't reopen every time someone mentioned the man. Granted, his father had placed the pack in this predicament in the first place. "Turns out, my father didn't want me as alpha, and he'd even stated as such in his last will and testament. I'm assuming, that's why the alpha challenge went the way it did. My brother and I faced off, and I'd had a clear advantage. But before I could put an end to the fight, the older folks in the pack interfered, driving me from the land."

"That's underhanded," Sierra spat. Her gaze flashed amber, her wolf surfacing. His teeth sharpened in response, the rage as fresh as it had burned mere months before. Her sympathy came as a surprise—based on the anger she'd greeted him with from the get-go, he hadn't expected any compassion. Yet, maybe more than anyone. she'd understand the burden of an alpha, the pride that came along with the title, and the fierce protectiveness he felt for his packmates.

He forced a bitter smile. "I thought so. My brother took ruthless advantage, claiming leadership over a pack he never rightfully won, which split us in two. The older folks aligned with him, but the rest of the pack broke off and followed me. We've just been fighting over land and leadership ever since. Those who defected with me are barred from our pack cabin, from the campgrounds belonging to Silver Springs, but they don't have enough force to oust us from our homes yet. I honestly couldn't tell you if my father's wishes stand up for a second in our kind's law—it's not like Drew won the alpha fight the way shifters are supposed to."

Sierra tilted her head to the side. "My earlier question remains. What brings you to our neck of the woods?"

Dax rolled his shoulders back. His skin prickled at all this admission, the whole affair making him feel more vulnerable than a cub. He hated it. "We need help. You want to talk reputations? You've earned one in this region for being smarter than most and right now brawn isn't what's going to win our land back. Smarts might."

"You've got a strange way of asking for help." Her voice came out dry.

"I don't want this territory, but I won't leave my pack without a home." Fierceness pulsed under the surface, the protectiveness he felt for each individual in his pack—for the misguided, wonderful lot who'd placed their faith in a fuck-up like him. "This land is the closest to the region my brother now holds hostage. If I can't find a way to undo the damage my father caused and unite our packs, we'll have no choice but to carve out our section of this region."

A growl came from Sierra's throat, as feral as her wolf.

Chapter Three

Control. Don't lunge at the cocky bastard to rip his throat out.

Sierra sucked in a deep breath to compose herself even though her wolf bucked forward, ready to tear into Dax, a man so stubborn he had done this entire exchange nude. Her pack thought she took top of the list on pride and stubbornness, but she had apparently met her match.

"Let me get this straight," she said, her voice coming out low and menacing. "You're telling me I either help you, or you attack me? That's not much of a sales pitch, sweetheart."

Dax shifted from where he stood, over six feet of tanned, delicious muscle that would make most women moan. Her irritation warred with a pulse of attraction she'd never admit aloud, and one that baffled her. She had her pick of the pack and plenty of strong, capable men to choose from, but despite scrapping with the boys and the occasional hookup, this magnetism hadn't descended in a long, long time. And she avoided that territory at all costs. Despite her best intentions, she couldn't help sneaking a glance his way.

An obnoxious smile reached his lips again as he fixed those cerulean eyes on her. "Who said I was finished?" He ran a hand through his dark ash strands, long enough to tug. "You don't think I'd be stupid enough to tramp down here and simply declare war, do you?"

Sierra lifted a brow.

A low laugh rumbled from him. "Fair enough."

"Then what's your proposal?" she asked.

"I'm coming to you and asking for an alliance," Dax responded, the shift of his hips drawing her eyes to traceable abs and a faint trail of dark hair directing her gaze down. "If you help me reunite my pack, we'll be a formidable force, one that will be indebted to you for life. Any threat coming into the region, any challenge to your authority, and I'll have your back."

Sierra pursed her lips, mulling over the offer. She preferred alliances with other wolves over cats, but she also couldn't handpick neighbors. Dax might be irritating as get all, but he'd been truthful with her so far and had tried to claim his leadership by honest means. Based on what she knew of Dax's father's history and his brother's reputation of being an aggressive asshole, taking a risk on Dax might be worth it, if he wanted to run the pack differently.

"How do I know your word is good?" she asked. So far Dax Williams had been an enigma, a meld of confidence mixed with vulnerability and a fighting spirit tempered by humility. After governing over a pack for as long as she had, she could navigate charged situations in her sleep. Still, she hadn't expected a straight answer from him, not after the way he'd goaded her earlier.

"I'll send one of my pack to live with you," he responded. "Even if it's in rotation, you'll have a Silver Springs pack member at your camp to utilize however you see fit." Those shrewd eyes met hers. "I trust you to be honorable in your usage." He leaned down to snag the clothes from the floor before slinking into the sweats and shirt she'd provided.

Too bad. The man painted a pretty picture, one she didn't mind viewing. She'd gotten an eyeful of how endowed he was, and the sight didn't help the adrenaline pulsing through her veins or the growing ache inside her. Maybe she would run some drills with Finn. She needed to blow some of this charged energy before it muddled her head.

"Do you happen to have a copy of your father's will? We'll need that and to take a trip to scope out the area." She rested her elbows on her knees, hunching forward. His pack's attack on him didn't stack up, but if they got the local shifter enforcers involve—or worse, the major power on this side of the country, the East Coast Tribe—all sorts of complications would arise. His brows furrowed in confusion, and a slow smile rose to her lips as their eyes met. Clarity descended in those too-pretty blues of his as he nodded, extending his palm to shake.

"Pleasure doing business with you, Kanoska," he said as she clapped her hand to his. Heat from his palm pressed against hers, and the husky tone of his voice didn't help as electricity crackled through her in one quick sweep. Hell on earth, she needed a swig of Jack, to sling a couple of punches or a tumble in the sheets with a packmate—and fast—if she reacted this way after a mere touch from the kitty-cat alpha.

"Glad you saw fit to join me in civility," she said with a smirk, giving him a once-over. His gaze glittered as he leaned over the coffee table and grabbed one of the notepads and pens splayed across the surface to scribble on the lined paper. He made his way to the exit, several strides of his powerful legs taking him across the linoleum, past the kitchen and the closed doors. Pausing by the doorframe, Dax tapped the side with his fingertips before turning to her.

"Give me a call. We can meet up tomorrow morning," he said, tilting his head in the direction of the number he'd left. "Or sooner, if you feel like getting uncivilized." He winked as he slipped out of the cabin, disappearing before the notepad smacked against the wall.

* * * *

Sierra called Dax Williams the second she hopped out of bed at sunrise. Apparently, he wasn't a morning person. After setting a time to meet and texting Jeremiah, she chugged her first two cups of coffee, annihilating the rest of her creamer in the process, and tossed on a heather-gray tank top and a pair of jeans with fewer rips than normal. Lastly, she strapped on her ass-kicker boots. A knock pounded on her door, as prompt as she'd expected.

"Come on in," she shouted, not bothering to head in and greet the arrival at the pack house. She set her coffee cup in the overflowing sink and walked through the cabin she spent most of her time in, ten minutes away from her tangled ivy cottage down the road, one she loved to pieces. The wooden floorboards creaked under her heavy boots as she made her way into the living room. The door flung open, and Jeremiah sauntered in, a loose bag slung over one shoulder and wearing a canvas vest with bulging pockets, more than a couple of Swiss Army knife handles peeking out.

"Remind me why we're helping this asshole again?" Jeremiah whined. She shot him a glare, eliciting a charming grin from the pretty man. As one of the taller pack members, he towered over her, his lanky frame hiding a deceptive amount of muscle. Based on his glossy chestnut waves and lashes long enough to make a model jealous, most dismissed him as a handsome face—their loss, because Streaky knew how to pack a punch.

"Because your darling alpha is a sucker for a sob story," she muttered, grabbing her own canvas bag from the floor. "And because we've gotten big enough to draw attention, but we don't have any alliances formed. As much as I'd like to say we could take 'em all on our own, protection of this pack comes first. If we gain a strong ally from this favor, the time will have been well spent."

Jeremiah snorted. "Still don't think cat shifters would be our best allies."

Sierra fixed him with a look that had his hands rising in defense as together they strode out the door. "Hence why I'm the alpha, and you're not."

She'd made unpopular decisions before and would again, but she always followed her gut. If she fucked up, she'd own her mistakes. Her gut instinct said Dax Williams and his merry band of kitty shifters told the truth. And as a fellow alpha, she could understand the agony at having a fight for leadership interrupted, the rage at the pack being split unfairly and the shame at having to slink to another pack for help.

Sierra locked up behind her while Jeremiah hopped in the driver's side of his jeep. He revved the engine as she joined him in the other seat, and with a rumble, they took off. Even though the early morning rays trickled down, the day already promised to be a sweltering one, and sweat pricked along her arms, making her wish she'd worn a looser tank top. Summers in Pennsylvania meant ample humidity, thickness she could suck through a straw.

Jeremiah pulled out onto the highway, and they set to flying, her hair streaming behind her and the sunshine pulsing a steady beat into her dark strands. The scent of motor oil tangled with the buttercups on the side of the road waving in the breeze, an intoxicating combination that enlivened her as much as the morning sun.

"We're not stomping into enemy territory, are we?" Jeremiah asked, his gaze slipping to hers.

"Stomping isn't what I had in mind—skating around it, maybe." Sierra leaned back in her seat, basking in the glow. "You're being brought along for your other skills."

Jeremiah began fanning himself with one hand, the other firm on the wheel. "Don't tell me you're here to drag me in front of a slew of lovely ladies?"

Sierra shot him a glare. "Get your head out of your ass. Like I need more of you proud peacocks strutting around."

Jeremiah snorted. "Aww, boss, I'm hurt. I'm guessing you need my lawyer expertise?"

"Bingo. You'll be looking over a will. Leave the sleuthing to those who can handle it," she teased. Hormones tended to rule among the Red Rock pack, whether hotheaded squabbles erupted over where someone parked their goddamn jeep, or someone slept with someone else's boyfriend. Either way, most of the time she felt more like the pack babysitter than any sort of alpha.

Up ahead, the rendezvous point came into view, a roadside diner with a paste-white sign so bright it glared amid the fringe of surrounding forest. Jeremiah screeched to a halt first, popping on his blinker a second before he turned into the lot of Zip's Diner. Red-and-white canopy decorated the length of the building to hover over the windows situated around the joint. The entire place stood no taller than one of the bigger cabins in Rickett's Glen State Park, with a sign that spanned half the length of the building.

"Our shifter friend has impeccable taste," Jeremiah said, his words coming out half-sneer. Not like Sierra blamed him—this place looked as inviting as a sewage plant. Yet the steady trickle of walker- and cane-accompanied folks coming in and out through the main doors was heartening, as was the packed parking lot. People were either satisfied or desperate.

"We're not going here for him to wine and dine us," Sierra responded, hopping out of the jeep before Jeremiah finished putting it into Park. Her boots thudded on the pavement and the sun winked at her, glancing off all the bumpers and chrome in the parking lot. She tugged her glossy hair into a ponytail while waiting for Jer to join her. A familiar figure leaned against the whitewashed wall of the building. Sierra didn't need to home in to tell who waited—she noticed his presence as she would one of her own pack.

Dax Williams sauntered toward her with feline grace, his eyes simmering with amusement the second they locked gazes. His jeans hung low on his hips, and his white tee might as well have been plastic-wrapped on, providing a clear reminder of the chiseled six-pack she'd seen last night.

"They've got some great kibble on the menu here," he drawled, eliciting a growl from Jeremiah. Her blood ignited. The man might be as pretty as a picture, but his smart-ass mouth ruined the package. Sierra contained her annoyance, offering a sweet smile while hiding her fangs.

"How considerate," she murmured.

His brows furrowed in confusion. If he wanted to play power games, now that her temper had cooled and she tapped into a clear perspective, he didn't stand a chance. She clapped a hand on Jeremiah's shoulder. He had bared his teeth, two steps away from wolfing out around more than a couple of humans in front of this quaint diner. Perfect recipe for freaking out the norms. Their eyes met, and she stared him down with her patented alpha look. Sure, her wolf paced restlessly inside her, desperate to establish dominance with the newcomer, but Sierra steered this ship for a reason.

"Lest you think I came for witty banter," Dax said as he made his way to the door and held it open for Jeremiah with a flourish. Jer folded his arms over his chest, refusing to budge. *Save me from fragile male egos.* Dax's eyes glittered with unspent amusement, clarifying that the gesture was meant as a taunt.

"Streaky, he's not asking you to marry him, just holding the door," Sierra said, giving Jer a shove hard enough to send him stumbling. She followed through, shooting a glare at Dax as she passed. "And you're no better. Taunting people you want help from is poor form. Shape up."

Dax's gaze darkened, and for a moment, she wasn't sure if they were headed for a brawl right in the parking lot. Not uncommon with her kind. His breath hitched for a half second, but as sudden as a swerving car, he flashed her a hot-as-hell smile.

"Yes, ma'am," he said, following them into the diner. Jer had already claimed a booth right in the corner—

best vantage point in the place—and he sat with his back to the outdated striped wallpaper. Sierra slid in beside him, and Dax sprawled out on the opposite bench. A waitress came bustling over, as hunched and withered as Sierra would expect from a place like this. Gray-stained teeth poked out with the woman's smile as she took drink orders. After ordering her third cup of coffee for the morning, Sierra followed the waitress back to the swinging doors to whisper an extra order.

Dax's gaze heated her the entire time. In fact, he'd watched her from the second they arrived. Her pack had more than a couple of attractive, eligible males, but apart from the infrequent hookup, they viewed her as off-limits. Most considered her one of the guys, and everyone else found her status intimidating. She'd learned that the hard way. The brazen look in Dax's eyes was new, as if he undressed her with his gaze.

Sierra slipped back onto the cracked vinyl of the booth as the waitress disappeared past the chrome swinging doors. "So whip out the goods," she said, eliciting a smirk from him. Before he could respond with a guaranteed annoying comment, she continued. "You brought the will?"

He passed the stack of papers to the center of the table. "Human lawyers wouldn't be the faintest lick of help in this situation, and no one in our pack practices law. So, I'm not sure if this spells out why the elders of the pack interfered in our match or not."

"I'll be able to gauge that quick," Jer murmured as he grabbed the documents. He'd already pulled his reading glasses out, thick black frames that hooked on his nose. The second the papers came into the picture, her packmate's lazy, domineering behavior vanished, all signs of his temper forgotten. With the will on the table, Jer's stare grew more focused, and his mouth pressed into a fine line as he scanned the hefty document. Even if he had broken so many pool sticks at Beaver Tavern over the years they added the expense to his tab, Sierra admired his professionalism. He was one of the best shifter lawyers in the region, and he'd chosen to run with the Red Rock pack.

"While he's going over the papers, I figured you and I could sleuth around my old territory so you can see firsthand what we're dealing with." Dax fiddled with the spoon on the table. He must not be comfortable asking for favors, but the man was willing to bury his pride for the sake of his pack.

"Good," she agreed, respect warming her chest. "We can scout out any areas the scent isn't heavy, see if we can sneak in and find why these elders interfered in the first place."

The waitress came out from the swinging doors, carrying a tray laden with the drinks and an opened can. "Going to place some orders?"

"Stuffed French toast for me," Sierra volunteered first, since her sweet tooth refused to be denied. Jer placed an order for a bacon-and-cheese omelet, while Dax went straight for the classic creamed chipped beef on toast with a side of scrapple.

The waitress placed the coffee in front of Sierra, two Cokes in front of the boys and the can in front of Dax. "Courtesy of your friend," the waitress said, directing a thumb at Sierra before darting away.

"Eat up, kitty cat," Sierra said sweetly, unable to help the smirk claiming her lips. This revenge tasted much sweeter than a simple retort or spark of temper. Dax's jaw dropped for a second as he stared at the opened can in front of him. "From what I hear," she continued, "this place is well known for their tuna."

He shook his head in disbelief, and his eyes sparked when they met hers. Until his shoulders started quaking, and a sharp laugh burst from him, surprising both Sierra and Jer. "See, smarts. That's why we came to you, Kanoska."

"Flattery won't get you anywhere," she muttered, even though a flush rose to her cheeks. The concession didn't satisfy as much as torment him, and she didn't quite trust the prickle of heat spreading from her cheeks to her nape in response. Dax winked before he tugged his fork out and began shoveling the contents of the tuna can into his mouth.

Jer's forehead creased when he glanced up from the papers. "You're actually eating that?"

Dax shrugged. "Why not? Still decent food, and I worked up an appetite after my morning run. Besides, we'll need fuel before Sierra and I get physical later," he said, the heat behind his voice making the suggestion quite clear. The sensuality of his statement traveled straight between her legs, a thrum begging for attention. Not that she'd indulge.

Jer didn't hold back the growl as he bared his teeth. "Don't you dare talk about my alpha that way."

Sierra squeezed Jer's shoulder. "Thanks for being all worried over my honor, but the mean ole kitty cat will have to try a lot harder if he wants to get a rise out of me." She fixed her gaze on Dax, challenge burning in her chest. "You worry about keeping up when we're out in the woods. Don't think I missed the way you had to catch your breath yesterday."

He smirked, pushing the empty can of tuna toward her. "Depends on what sort of exertion we're talking about."

She shot him a glare in response.

In a matter of minutes, the waitress stepped in, bringing a tray full of food. Not like Sierra didn't enjoy verbally sparring with Dax, but the man had a way of getting under her skin, and she didn't trust the way her body reacted to him. The scents of syrup and cinnamon drifted her way, combined with the salty tang of meat, the crisp char of toast and strong coffee.

The table lapsed into silence as they scarfed down food. With all the energy she burned while running in wolf form, she'd better get her calories in now. Dax and Jer dug in with equal gusto, and in minutes the plates had been emptied apart from a couple of crumbs. Once the waitress had cleared the plates, Dax broke the silence.

"Since the niceties are now over, let's get down to business," he said, tossing a couple of crisp bills onto the table. "We've got territory to scout."

"If our exchange until now is what you'd call niceties, no wonder your pack's in trouble," Sierra muttered, eliciting a razor grin from him. She added her crumpled cash to the table and squeezed Jer's shoulder. "I'll keep you informed. Thank you for helping me with this."

He glanced over to Dax then back at her, distrust clear in his eyes. "Call me if you need anything."

Sierra nodded and took the lead toward the exit. "Let's go for a run."

Chapter Four

Dax surged past Sierra in the parking lot, guiding them towards his truck. He came to a stop in front of his truck, a sleek black beauty that had gotten him out of more scrapes than he could count. Wind rattled the tarp over the bed of the truck, which covered bags of cement leftover from his last contractor job.

"Hop on in," he said, unlocking the car and slipping into the driver's seat. The second he turned the ignition, the powerful engine thrummed under him, a wisp of control amid all this family bullshit he'd now dragged the Red Rock pack into. He rolled down the windows before gliding out of the parking lot and entering the highway.

Sierra leaned out the window, her forearm pressed against the frame as the breeze tangled strands of her long ponytail. Already the sun promised a scorching day and blossoming sweat glued his tee to his chest. He tugged at the neck, gripping the steering wheel with the other hand as he zoomed across the asphalt, making his way to the place he'd grown up, the home and people he thought he'd known until they'd exiled him.

"How many folks stayed?" Sierra's voice cut through the darker thoughts beginning to crop up.

"About a dozen," he responded, brushing away the couple of strands of hair plastered to his forehead. "Most of the elders, the toughest, weathered members of the pack. The whole thing tore families apart, since the other half came with me. They're waiting for me to make a move on Drew and the others, but if this is our pack's civil war, I'd rather settle this between Drew and me than let the rest of the pack get bloody in the process. Our best chance might be making enough noise to draw the Tribe to the region."

Sierra formed her lips into a thin line as she nodded. Any alpha knew what complications could arise by grabbing the attention of the governing group of shifters who ruled over the entire East Coast. Drag them into this dispute, and the entire Silver Springs pack was liable to be punished for their inability to self-govern. His father had left a legacy of trouble, of a disregard for the honor his people were supposed to uphold.

"Jer's the best at what he does," Sierra said. "If your father's will holds any weight among the pack, he'll be able to figure it out."

He pressed on the gas pedal, hurtling ahead. As prickly as she'd been on their first meeting, he'd warmed up to Sierra Kanoska faster than he liked. She strode into a room with command, yet had the wry humor to tease back, to indulge in the games his feline side loved, and her heart was big enough to offer reassurance at the right time. He understood at once why her wolf pack followed her with such a fierce devotion.

Shame flushed through him at his own splintered front. Sure, the cats who'd separated would back him with their last breath, but he couldn't help but wonder if a stronger leader could've kept the pack together. Somehow.

Familiar highway markers flashed into view, green-and-white exit signs he'd seen a thousand and one times, yet now he entered the area as an intruder, a stranger in his own home. Even if his brother's splitting of the pack hadn't made the area dangerous territory, the betrayal of pack members Dax had grown up with and considered aunts and uncles sliced him too deeply to move past.

The silent brooding he'd slipped into came to a close with the way Sierra kept glancing his way. His pride wouldn't allow her to witness him sulking around like some kid. "You seem to keep finding excuses to get me alone," Dax purred, slipping into avoidance mode.

Sierra's gaze hardened and she jutted her jaw forward. "Anyone ever mention you've got a one-track mind? No wonder you need my help figuring out a solution to your problem."

The jab sank home, piercing his tough-as-shit shell and driving straight into the meat of his current insecurities. His gaze flared, and his grip on the wheel tightened. "I'm not the one who's buzzing with pent-up sexual frustration. What's the matter? Scare too many men out of your bed?"

She didn't respond, but judging by how her lips pressed tightly and the claws pricked from her nails, he'd crossed a line. He'd encountered a great many who sparked his temper before, but rarely did anyone challenge him like she did. "What's the matter?" he added, unable to resist himself. "Cat got your tongue?"

"Go to hell," Sierra snapped. "Maybe you'll find some more original material there." Her dark eyes blazed with her irritation, and a fine line formed between her brows while she frowned at him. Poking the bear—or the wolf in this case—wasn't in his best interest, but since she'd proven herself to be as prideful as he was, he didn't believe for a second she'd dive into a care-and-share on why his comment pissed her off.

Ahead, a thick grove of oaks, birches and sugar maples swarmed the horizon, a forest he'd raced through from early on and memorized every square inch of. His mother used to scruff him as a cub, dragging him back home from these woods when he'd run off. After her sunshine-and-steel presence had faded away due to ovarian cancer, none of the males in their family had quite recovered.

Dax slowed and pulled onto an unpaved turnoff, one the pack used. Shade devoured them in a heartbeat, from the overhang of the thick, lush oaks towering above the others. Being around here set his nerves at a constant simmer, and he wasn't the only one. Sierra's gaze burned holes into the back of his head.

Not like he'd go slinking in with his head bowed, but he needed her help and he needed her focused. As he settled into Park, he winked at her. "Maybe your wolf pups are scared to tangle with a strong woman, but, darling, I'd devour you." Heat flooded his voice.

Even though the intensity of her gaze hadn't lessened, he didn't miss the way her tongue glided over those fuck-me lips and how she shifted in her seat. Her copper skin didn't betray a blush, but he'd hazard a guess other parts heated in response.

"Nice to know you're focused," she shot back, the sharpness from before leaving her tone.

His grin widened. "It's what I'm known for. Now, stop wasting all this time flirting with me. We've got a job to do." Before she could respond, he hopped out of his truck and closed the door. A growl came from Sierra's side as she slunk from her seat and slammed the car door shut with extra emphasis—enough to make the frame of his truck reverberate. The woman had a formidable temper, but most shifters did—especially other alphas.

"So, we're in enemy territory now, yes?" Sierra asked, striding past him toward the woods. "Meaning, anyone we might encounter around here will view us as hostile?"

"Yes, ma'am," he said with a lazy salute as he kept pace. "We're here to poke around and see if we overhear anything. If there's unrest at my brother's camp, we may be able to push at the dissenting ones rather than needing to bring things to the Tribe."

"And rather than bringing your own pack for this highly dangerous mission, you're trusting me?" she asked, stopping her tread to face him. "Unless this is a trap and you're looking to eliminate competition."

Dax let out a slow exhale. "I understand the distrust, so I'll be clear with you—my motives in bringing you aren't a hundred percent pure. If my pack shows up and we're discovered, it'll be an instant fight, no questions asked."

Sierra nodded with her arms crossed in front of her and her shrewd eyes always analyzing. "It's one thing fighting against your old pack members but another fighting a war on two fronts. Enough to make anyone hesitate. And you're bringing the alpha of an outsider pack in a very clear statement," she murmured, her brows lifting. "Clever move."

Praise from her sank into his bones, giving him confidence he'd been missing. She had a way about her, a blunt honesty that didn't trifle with false flattery or wasted words. Sierra fascinated him—that much he didn't bother denying. Even though he flirted with her to get a rise, he had to admit he relished the idea of tangling with someone as powerful and gorgeous as the wolf alpha.

"Leave your clothes here," he said, jerking a thumb near his car. "We'll pick them up on our way out." With the swiftness he expected, she shucked her clothes to the ground, and he followed suit. They continued walking until they reached the end of the unpaved road leading into the woods where amber rays of escaped sunlight glowed through the tree branches.

"Follow me," he directed, letting the shift roll through him.

His skin rippled, the fur spreading over his skin and his canines dropping as he shifted into the mountain lion. Nature sprawled out more vibrantly than before, like when the Wizard of Oz changes from black and white to Technicolor. The wild part of him purred in contentment to pad through these woods again.

Just as fast, Sierra transformed into the sleek wolf he'd run with the other day. Her amber eyes glowed as she paced back and forth, waiting for him to lead the way. Her silver fur soaked in the shadows of the forest, dappled patterns splaying on her coat. Despite the normal distance the predators would keep, his cat didn't find her wolf repulsive. She smelled like sunshine and cinnamon, a warm blend that caused his nostrils to flare.

He traveled down trails he had scampered with his brother so many years ago. Before their mom had passed away and before his father's aggressive, competitive nature fractured their relationship into pieces that couldn't be glued back together. When they were kids, only the give of soft earth under their paws and the amber beams of the summer sun warming their fur mattered. Drew was a big brother he'd loved and looked up to once upon a time, and despite the damage between them, those memories always tangled his conviction.

These power games, the fierce battle for leadership, all while fresh dirt covered their father's grave, cast a darker shade to these lands. A cool chill settled over him, even as he scanned the area for any sign of his old pack. Sierra kept pace with ease, the determined gaze on her wolf the same one that furrowed her brow when she spoke in an imperious, commanding tone. For all that he'd just met the woman, she'd made quite the mark in his mind.

Her ears pricked to attention at the same time he caught a faint rattling in the distance. He slowed to a trot, each step silent when they approached a sparser section of the woods. The oak trunks thinned, the sandstone and shale grew more frequent and large patches of grass, moss and stray leaves claimed the area. He'd spent his teenage years tossing back the bottles of Jack he had stolen from his dad and getting down and dirty with the females in the pack at the Cove, an old, well-used clearing.

He tilted his head to Sierra before glancing ahead, hoping she took the cue to stay a few paces behind. He didn't want to get her injured in a surprise attack—better she approach once he established his presence.

Sierra dipped her muzzle in response and slowed to a halt. *Good.* Time to investigate what idiot was tromping through these woods with such a thunder even a human could catch his or her trail.

His heart thudded in his chest, not from fear, but the anticipation for a fight. The choking futility of his situation crawled under his skin in a real way, and while teasing Sierra helped him blow off a little steam, he had a lot more irritation to burn. Dax padded closer, careful to keep his scent off the breeze by prowling low to the ground. Voices drifted his way, a firm baritone and a light and soft female one, both of which he recognized.

"—needs to put on a stronger front," hissed Rylie, one of the older females who'd abandoned him in favor of his brother.

"The Tribe's taking notice," the baritone replied, the voice belonging to his Uncle Aiden. Dax's chest grew tight at the sound. Out of all the betrayals, that one hurt the worst. He and his father might have had a strained relationship at best, but Uncle Aiden had been the dad his own never was, the guy who had taught him how to fight, to shift and to think like a mountain lion. Except when the elders had turned on Dax, Aiden had stepped aside out of respect to the old man.

"Andrew needs to bring Dax and the others in line before the disruption brings enforcers breathing down our neck, or worse, the Tribe to town. This whole situation could leave our pack and territory up for grabs." Rylie paced back and forth, tall, lean and with deeper bags under her eyes than Dax remembered. Uncle Aiden cast a long shadow along the mossy ground with his arms folded and his face grim.

"If Drew isn't strong enough to hold these lands and smart enough to bring the pack together, maybe we aligned ourselves with the wrong alpha," he said.

Dax let out a light huff of breath at the statement. A trickle of relief coursed through him—his uncle hadn't lost faith in him after all. Sierra stalked beside him, so silent her presence barely registered.

Uncle Aiden's nose twitched, and his eyes were flashing umber as he glanced in their direction. "I smell wolf."

Dax's muscles coiled as he readied to run.

Until a snarl sounded behind them.

He whipped around at the sound, his hackles rising and a roar of his own ripping through the air. A golden-furred mountain lion prowled their way, the silver eyes and couple of spots a clear indicator the newcomer was his old packmate, Ben. Sierra vibrated with her returning growl, her muscles tensed with coiled violence ready to unload.

Red steamed Dax's vision, rage that flooded through his veins like the dose of adrenaline. He lunged for Ben, distracting him from Sierra. His old packmate didn't hesitate, meeting him for the charge. Ben swiped a claw at his face, but he wove around the attempt, balancing on his pads for fast, quick motion. Dax pivoted, slamming his skull into Ben's side with enough force to knock him back. His head rattled against the shifter's ribcage right as a low snarl came from behind him from the uncle he'd fought a thousand times before. He whipped around to face the impending threat.

"We made a promise to Martin," Rylie snarled at him, her claws pricking out. "His blood son should take the mantle, and you don't qualify."

Dax's heart stilled. Despite the stagnant humidity, cold leeched through him at an alarming rate. He didn't want to think about the complicated mess the fight for alpha had turned into. He didn't want to think about the brother he'd once known so well. Most of all, he didn't want to think about his fucking father and the secrets he'd taken with him to the grave.

Rylie's human form disappeared, and in her place prowled a hulking mountain lion. Rylie's coat was colored gray like ash, while Uncle Aiden towered over them, larger than most of the Silver Springs shifters. All three focused on him, smart enough to not tangle with the wolf intruder until they sussed out where she'd come from. Before he could pick a target, a thud to his side sent him tumbling. Ben leaped on top of him, those jaws snapping an inch from his throat.

The heft of the other cat should've kept him pinned, but Dax had maneuvered his way out of worse. He struck at the back of the closest leg pinning him down, his sharp claw slicing at the tendon. Ben yowled as he moved his weight to the other side. With the imbalance, Dax's opening emerged. He shoved forward, pushing Ben over with a thud. Once he lunged free, bursting out onto the ground, Uncle Aiden appeared.

He rammed into Dax's side, the force of the blow sending him flying. Dax tumbled to the ground, the air whooshing from his lungs as he found his grip, his claws sinking into the dirt. Not like he'd be able to catch a breath. Rylie closed the feet between them, pure murder glowing in those eyes.

Until a silver wolf met her midway, slamming right into her.

Rylie went tumbling. Sierra let out a snarl and darted toward him. Ben swiped at her, a lazy sort meant to dismiss, not maim—poor bastard, poking the beast. The wolf's amber eyes glowed as she regarded her prey before he'd even realized the tornado he'd unleashed.

Dax seized the distraction, circling to face Uncle Aiden. Those dark eyes glared down on him as his uncle padded around, patient as he searched for the right opening. The man had the weight and the skill to take Dax out with one blow, and worse, he had taught him all the tricks he knew. His head throbbed, adrenaline pounding through him. Rylie had already wobbled to her feet and she zoned in on him, wrath glowing in her eyes.

He lunged in, directing his head to the left. Uncle Aiden rose to respond, striking out as Dax collided with him. Right before Uncle Aiden sent him tumbling, he flexed his claws, sinking them into flesh. He focused on the grip before gravity took over, and he rolled away to slam against the ground. His right leg tugged against the hold he had, the old fishing hook routine his uncle had shown him so often before. He scrambled to unhook, his uncle letting out a loud rumble as Dax pushed himself from the ground on his front paws. A furry blur sailed overhead.

Rylie had pounced.

Her claws sank deep, biting past the fur and sinking into tissue. She raked down, scoring along his ribcage. Pain swept through him in a fierce, stinging sweep, enraging him even more. Her claws descended again, but this time he was ready. Dax bashed his head against her front leg, sending her recoiling, but he didn't step away. Instead, he lunged, his jaw clicking as he snapped his teeth at her.

Uncle Aiden rammed into him from the side again.

Dax thudded against the ground, his breaths coming out in a hiss. Blood streamed from the cut, mingling with the loose dirt. He rose to his legs regardless. Rylie raced for him again, her front claws stained with his blood and promising to tear in for more. With him out of the way, the rest of the pack might rejoin under Drew's rule. They could go to hell. He steadied himself, ready to surge ahead.

Until Sierra whipped into view, slamming into their way.

Rylie smashed into her, sending her tumbling to the ground. But the bitch was out for blood, and she lashed out with those claws, red staining Sierra's pristine silver fur. Dax's blood pounded through him in a furious pulse. Not thinking, not processing, he charged.

Before he landed, Uncle Aiden threw himself in the way, shoving Rylie off Sierra. Dax skidded to a halt in front of her, avoiding his uncle by an inch. A snarl ripped from Uncle Aiden's lips as he bumped Rylie in the direction of the woods. Ben dipped his muzzle and took off, weaving past the trees. Rylie let out a low growl before she slunk away from Sierra, and Uncle Aiden followed, the three of them disappearing as fast as they'd arrived.

Sierra staggered to her feet, red trickling through her coat. The sight made Dax rage all over again, a fierce thud in his chest scrambling his senses. She nudged his neck, directing him to the path they'd come from. He dipped his head in agreement, and they took off.

Chapter Five

Sierra reached the car first, padding around to the passenger side before shifting back into human form. The second she did, she wished she'd remained in the stronger form since pain radiated all across her side from the cat bitch's vicious gouges. She sucked in a deep breath, blood leaking from her wounds at a pace she didn't like. Had to get something to stop up the flow.

The car door clicked open, and a second later a towel flew her way. She wrapped it around herself, pressing her hand against the oozing cut before she slipped into the passenger seat. Even though Dax had tossed their crumpled clothes in the back, she preferred to clean bloodstains off a towel than destroy yet another pair of jeans. Dax had already settled into the driver's seat, blood staining the leather. He turned on the ignition and glanced her way, his blue eyes scorching with concern.

"My place isn't far from here. We'll clean your wound there, and you can borrow some clothes," he said, not quite meeting her eyes. The guilt was a new look on him, one she didn't quite like seeing.

"I'm not the only one dripping blood all over the seats," she mentioned, keeping her palm pressed against the wound. The bloodstain spread across the tan towel she wore. Dax hadn't bothered to drape himself in anything or even try to stop the bleeding from his scratches as he tore down the gravel path. Not like she minded the view—the coiled muscles, the lethal frame and his lickable, sun-kissed skin fueled the reminder she hadn't gotten laid in far too long.

His truck soared along the highway, pine and oak trees surrounding them on either side as they headed into the next town over, another half-mile strip of shops visible in the distance.

"I'm sorry," he said, his voice gruff as his gaze focused on the road ahead. His jaw tightened at the same time his grip on the steering wheel did. "You shouldn't have gotten hurt back there. I shouldn't have dragged you into this mess."

"What's this? Didn't think you feline types had apologies in you," she responded, forcing a smile. "I didn't expect this to be a skip through the meadow, and I've gotten my share of scratches before. Quit beating yourself up and make sure when I cash in my favor you're in a position to help."

He snorted, pressing harder on the gas as they whizzed past a beat-down pharmacy and the sort of dive bar promising stale, watery beer and stained wallpaper. "Are you actually being nice, Kanoska?" he teased, his gaze lighting up. "All the blood loss must be messing with your head."

She shot him daggers, but his response didn't stir her irritation as it had a mere day ago. Witnessing his serious side gave her a glimpse into his constant needling—all a distraction to keep his distance, and probably for sanity's sake, given his current situation. The highway shifted into narrower roads, the asphalt less taken care of as he turned onto a rambling side street, one degraded to gravel. The sun winked overhead, glancing over every chrome curve of his truck.

As they both lapsed into silence, she stole another glance. Despite his distracting body, she found herself staring at the light scruff along his angular chin, the thick brows furrowed in concentration and the nick of a scar on his cheek. He had the long, sweeping lashes to place him in the "pretty" category, highlighting eyes that glowed blue when he shifted.

He turned down another side road, this one in the thick of the woods and not even making a pretense at civilization. His earlier words and the glint of interest in his eyes slithered down her spine, causing heat to flush through her despite the pain in her side. Her wound throbbed, but she'd received worse in her day. If she fainted over a couple of scratches, she'd lose any cred as an alpha. He wasn't the only one who had pride to uphold.

At the end of an unpaved driveway lay a small cabin composed of flat tan panels, wide windows, and a stone chimney rising in the back. A wide porch stretched across the front, strewn with a few wooden rocking chairs over the cherry-stained wood and a couple of steps led to the door. He sprayed gravel as he pulled in to park before switching off the ignition. She didn't miss the way his hand swung to the leaking scratches at his side as he slid out of the driver's seat.

Sierra hopped out, hiding her wince as she kept her palm pressed tightly to the slices refusing to clot. The tan towel turned into full-blown period horror mode, a growing splash of red that wouldn't come out anytime soon. Dax sauntered to the front of the house, keys jangling in his hand with his steady strides. He cast a glance at her, those blue eyes flashing with concern again.

"Come on in," he called as he fiddled with the door. She walked up the steps behind him, his tight, muscled ass on full display.

"Is this where you invite me in for a drink?" she asked, unable to help the grin curling her lips.

He cocked a brow, a rich smile returning to his face. "Sure, if that means you'll be joining me in bed later."

Even as irritation warmed her chest, it mingled with a heat spreading between her legs. He entered the cabin, and she followed, eager to clean and bandage her wound. The musk of cedar descended the second she stepped in, from the carved table and chairs in the center of the expansive gathering room to his kitchen countertops. An assortment of bowls cluttered his sink and a couple of jagged hunting knives dried on a towel along the countertop.

Overhead, a lighting fixture framed by antlers accented the woodsy home, and more than a couple of woolen blankets draped along the tan futon and long chestnut couch stretching the length of the back wall. Dax disappeared into one of the side rooms while she wandered over to the couch, hoping the dark fabric wouldn't collect the stains her towel had. She assumed he wasn't dicking around in there and had snagged some bandages. Despite the act he put on, Dax proved to be a lot smarter than most might give him credit for.

He emerged from his room, arms laden with gauze, antiseptic and a crumpled ball of clothing. He'd tossed on a pair of loose flannel pants but hadn't bothered with a shirt. Not like she minded. Blood trickled from his scratches, but he swiped his side, making the liquid smear across his skin, as he took a seat on the ottoman in front of her.

"Take off your towel," he said, unscrewing the antiseptic. He then tossed the ball of clothing on the couch beside her, a grin lighting his face. "You can join us civilized folks once you listen, like a good girl."

Sierra ground her teeth, her hands balling into fists and the urge to punch him rising. His gaze darkened for a microsecond, telltale of more brewing beneath the surface with him than the flirty persona he presented.

"Pass over the antiseptic and I'll do it myself," Sierra challenged.

He shook his head. "I got you into this mess. The least I can do is take care of you now," he said, lapsing into seriousness for once. "But as it stands, I can't get to the wound."

She heaved a sigh and undid her towel. Pain flared fiercely as she peeled the fabric from where she'd been pressing on those scratches. The tinny tang of blood filled the air and the shredded skin throbbed. Dax pulled a chair up, his brows knitting together in concentration as he splashed antiseptic on a smooth gauze pad. She settled her bare feet flat against the hardwood floor, bracing for the sting. He glanced at her, and she nodded.

When the soaked gauze descended, Sierra let out a hiss. She focused on Dax, trying to ignore the pain. This close, his woodsmoke smell wrapped around her, so similar to the cedar of this cabin. Despite her bravado, she was quite aware of her own nudity and how her body awakened around him. His lips pressed together as he tended to the wound. Like this, she glimpsed the Silver Spring alpha side of him, someone lethal and strong enough for part of his pack to split off to follow rather than indulging in his late father's corruption.

His hands remained steady as he cleaned her wounds, the tendons of those corded forearms bulging with each swipe. Heat pooled between her legs, despite the pain. Her body reacted to him with a thrill she hadn't experienced in a long while. Those years before when she thought she'd found the one, the bastard had fucked off when she'd become alpha, unable to accept her dominance. After that, she'd closed the door on relationships, sticking to tried and true flings.

With a few deft swipes, Dax attached a swath of gauze over the wound with pieces of medical tape. He placed a hand on the top of her bare thigh, the contact a jolt. Heat flooded through her, and her body pulsed with need from the single touch.

"You're all set," he said, rising off the couch. She snagged the ball of clothes he'd given her. Sierra tugged on the black T-shirt, which dwarfed her, and a pair of gray sweats she had to tighten the drawstrings on. Her nose wrinkled on instinct and her wolf paced inside her in protest. His scent marked these clothes so strongly she was drowning in it, stoking her predatory need to dominate and establish her own space. She'd forgotten her own clothes in his truck. The sound of running water came from the kitchen, and minutes later, Dax emerged with a matching gauze patch.

Her heart pounded in her ears from the thrill of the fight, the blood pumping hot through her veins. The sarcastic alpha in front of her wasn't helping diminish the blaze. Sierra perched on the edge of the couch, her elbows braced against her knees.

"So, what did you find out?" she asked. "Anything worth throwing ourselves out there like chum?" A glance at the clock told her they'd made decent time, which meant Jeremiah wouldn't be sending a search party out yet. Still, the boys would lose their shit if they figured she'd gotten mucked up in the scuffle. Despite the fact she could thrash their asses, they were an overprotective bunch, like the brothers she always wanted.

Dax sauntered toward her, his presence distracting like an itch she couldn't scratch. He sank into the couch inches from her, spreading his arms out along the back. This close, he emanated warmth, giving summer's humidity a run for its money.

"I found out they're screwed if the Tribe pays us a visit, so I'm about ready to bring the hellfire down on us. Can't be worse than the mess my pack's made of itself after Pops passed." He ran a hand through his dark strands, his smile flickering to serious. Darkness lingered in those blue eyes, as though ghosts haunted him, despite only the two of them standing in this cabin.

"Bring it," Sierra said with a shrug. Even though the Tribe ruled with a harsh hand, she understood the responsibility that came with their role and the burdens associated. She'd made her own unpopular calls for the betterment of her pack in the past, this being one of them.

"You're not what I expected, you know that?" he said, letting out a laugh as he clasped his hands behind his head.

She cocked an eyebrow. "And what were you expecting?"

"Based on the rumors, an ice queen with an iron fist. But you're vibrant, strong and fiercer than I ever anticipated." He cast a glance her way, his eyes twinkling with his smile. The lust in his gaze didn't surprise her but his intensity did. "The rumors failed to mention how devastatingly hot the Red Rock alpha happened to be too."

Her fingers curled into the cushion of the sofa at the statement. At the desire in his eyes. Sierra couldn't afford complications, not in her position, but the way he flirted with her and teased had amped her touch hunger to a deafening roar. He nudged her with his thigh, their knees bumping against each other. Her heart pounded in double time, and the wolf inside her snapped at the leash, ready to lunge in and sate her needs.

"You're all talk, Williams," she tossed back, the dare flaring inside her. The surge of attraction sparking through her hadn't risen to this crescendo in a long time.

His grin widened, reaching those wicked, teasing eyes as he leaned in closer. "If I didn't know better, I'd say that was a taunt." The air between them thickened with charged particles, ready to ignite. "Careful, sweetheart. I love a challenge."

The scent of cedar surrounded her, smothered her, his musk revving her engines with a surprising intensity. Her wolf lunged in her chest, desperate to mark, and Sierra's thighs tingled in response, her entire body prickling under the sweep of his gaze. He stared at her as if he wanted to devour her, his big body braced for action of a different sort. Each breath arrived shallower and the desire to taste those lips reached a rising beat in her chest.

She lifted her chin, meeting his gaze. He wanted to invite the storm in. She'd ravage him if only to knock the cocky smirk off his face.

Warmth spread inside her and she hid a secret grin as she lunged forward.

Despite the sting of her injuries, she descended on him with the fury of a wolf, her lips claiming his in one swoop. Dax's hands wrapped around her waist as he sank into the kiss, responding with similar aggression. He tasted like mint, and the second his lips parted, she slipped her tongue in. His palms heated through her shirt, fiery imprints branding her body. Dax tugged her toward him with one powerful swing, pulling her onto his lap.

She settled her thighs around his, her core throbbing with demand and her folds already slick and ready. From the way his erection pressed against her through the fabric, he was, too. Her mouth crashed against his again and again as she grew addicted to the minty taste, the smooth glide of his lips. He nipped at her lower lip, the bite sparking through her system like electricity. But Dax didn't stop there. After he pulled away for a breath, his mouth descended on the slope of her neck, teeth scraping against the sensitive skin.

The man had a clever mouth—she couldn't deny that.

The urge to claim reached a pulsing roar inside her. Her wolf tugged at her chest, lunging forward in a way she'd never experienced before. She'd thought the power wars with another alpha had sparked this intense fight in her. As his touch lit her inside, she wasn't so sure anymore.

Mine. Mine. Mine.

The words pounded in her blood, in her bones, until she lost herself in the heat of his hands, the scrape of his teeth and the glide of his lips. She sank her nails into his arms as the meaning of those words hit home.

Normal humans might get a little possessive, but for shifters, one thing inspired this sort of territorial edge. The sort of tug that reached soul deep with the promise of something real, something permanent. The mating bond.

Dax's eyes widened right as she pulled away, her throat going dry. Even though her wolf lunged forward inside her, desperate to complete the cycle and claim absolutely, Sierra, the human, the alpha, was not ready to make forever commitments with a man she barely knew.

She slipped off him with wolfish swiftness, her lips tingling and the bite on her neck where he'd sunk his teeth raw and brazen. Several scratches adorned his arms from her nails sinking into his skin, the claws pricking past in her shock. He regarded her with the caution of a predator. Apparently, she wasn't the only one smacked in the face with the realization. The closeness, the heat that had risen between them mere moments ago, extinguished. The mating bond had tossed a bucket of cold water on those mounting feelings.

Even so, her wolf rammed in her chest at the same anxious pulse as her heart. If she didn't get out of here, all logic would get thrown by the wayside, and animal nature would take over. The same nature that repeated *claim, claim, claim* in her head and in her heart.

"I've got to go." The words escaped from her without a second thought as she raced for the door. The second she burst into the fragrant summer air, the shift took over. When her padded feet hit the ground, Sierra ran.

Chapter Six

Mate.

Dax didn't do serious relationships. He'd never bothered with them because all those sparks flashed out of existence quickly and he'd move to the next fireworks display. He ran a hand through his short hair, sinking into the couch as if the soft cushions would devour him whole. As if his head wasn't already a cluster of confusion, the last thing he needed was this dropped bomb.

Sierra Kanoska had lit his veins on fire, and sure, he'd wanted to fuck her senseless the moment they'd met, but sating his aggression with a quick tumble was a different scenario than taking his mate to bed. Not like a guy just plucked one of those off the aisle. Some folks married happily, never finding their mate, but those lucky enough to find their fated had the partnerships his kind revered. The mating bond might take a while to develop or it could emerge from the outset—for them, they'd been cursed with the latter.

"Fuck me," Dax groaned before pushing off the suffocating grip of the couch. He barely knew Kanoska, and the words they'd exchanged had been filled with more than a little rancor. She would rip his heart out of his chest with her bare teeth and take his balls as a trophy over being his mate. She'd made her stance clear when she had bolted out of his house as if her tail was lit on fire. Not like he didn't agree—they'd just met. Those sorts of attachments bordered on lunacy.

Yet he needed her help. They'd left Jeremiah at the diner to go over the will, and if Dax's pack had turned on him because he was a bastard, he'd need all the support he could get to try to stake a fair claim as alpha. Alpha status had never been a dynasty, but after his father won the position after his father passed, the man had died trying to make it so.

Dax stalked into his room to put on a pair of pants without an elastic waistband. Whether she liked it or not, Kanoska had agreed to work with him, and he would hold her to her promise. Even if they had problems keeping their hands off each other and she happened to be his destined mate. No biggie. He tugged on a beat-up tee as he let out a long breath. Hell, he hadn't stayed in a relationship longer than six months, and in stomped a woman he barely knew with *lifetime potential* stamped all over her perfect ass.

He snagged his Flyers cap from his end table. The mating bond wasn't some arranged marriage. Both parties had to consent for the connection to solidify. After the pair confirmed the mating bond, most had a Tribe member bless the union through the totem spirits, similar to a wedding ceremony, but he'd only been to a couple in his lifetime. Those celebrations were massive, the sort to draw surrounding packs and unite a whole region together—the exact sort of chaos he wanted to avoid. Since she'd started out with a lower-than-average opinion of him, all he had to do was keep from falling for her.

His stomach churned at the thought. Easy as a run through the woods.

* * * *

For the second night in a row, he showed up at Beaver Tavern.

Wolf sweat drenched this little woodsy shithole of a bar, but he'd left Kyle and Ally at this bar last night to mingle, and they'd somehow escaped without a scratch. He, on the other hand, had managed to get more than a couple of scratches from a certain wolf alpha in the heat of the moment. The amber lights glowed with a welcome he wouldn't receive, not after what happened earlier in his cabin. Sierra must've run the whole way back, too, as he hadn't needed to deal with Jeremiah, the overprotective werewolf, banging on his door.

His jeans were wrinkled and his T-shirt torn in more than a couple of places, but he didn't bother with nice attire when the Red Rock alpha had bolted from his place earlier. With the way his luck was going lately, she'd call the whole deal off, and he'd be up shit creek. Dax heaved a sigh as he shoved his hands into his pockets and strolled to the entrance.

Shouts and laughter washed over him once he stepped inside, the scent of wet dog mingling with stale beer and unfinished wood. Even though he crept in at a silent tread, once he crossed the threshold, all eyes turned to him. Wolves and their keen noses.

He ignored the pressure of the stares leveled his way as well as the growls from the guys on the periphery who found his mere presence a threat. Not his problem if they grappled with insecurity.

Dax didn't even need to scan the place—he felt her there, another bad sign she'd imprinted on him more than he anticipated. Like déjà vu, Sierra Kanoska sat at the bar, a bottle in her hand, though this time, a hulking guy with a buzz cut stood behind the counter, rather than the vixen from yesterday. Dax approached the bar, remaining silent. With the way her shoulders tensed, he didn't need to announce his presence. She had the same awareness too.

He slid into the seat beside Sierra, the worn legs of the stool creaking as he settled. Unlike the hush from last night, though, folks were muttering crap under their breath and stealing sips from their pints.

The guy behind the bar flattened his palms on the surface, watching him with the wary eyes of a predator. "Give me one reason I shouldn't gut you here."

Dax didn't bat an eye, sliding out a pack of mints from his pocket. "First off, take the edge off your mutt breath before you go baring your teeth at me," he responded. The surly bartender's reached lightning fast across the counter to bat the pack of mints away and it smacked against the wall. Dax had to hide his smirk of amusement at how fast wolves' tempers sparked.

He angled his body to Sierra. "We made an agreement, which I haven't done anything to violate. So, unless the honor of the Red Rocks is as mythical as your patience, you won't be launching into an attack."

Sierra placed a hand on the barkeep's shoulder, giving it a squeeze. A flare of heat seared Dax at the casual touch she offered another guy. He exhaled slowly, calming the irrational impulse. Then the Red Rock alpha fixed those vibrant, dark eyes on him. His gut kicked with surprising strength. Hell, if making out with Kanoska inspired this sort of shit, he was screwed if they ever got down and dirty.

"I apologize," she said, loud enough for the bartender to hear. Her eyes locked with Dax's, the gravity in her expression snaring him on the spot. He understood at once she referred to earlier. At running when they needed to talk things out. Her lips were pursed and those deep eyes serious, but even though he wished he could tap into her current, her thoughts remained unreadable. "You didn't do anything to warrant hostility from my pack. If they can't behave," she said, casting a warning eye around the room, "then I'll have to assign them tasks to blow off all their extra energy."

At once, a clamor of shuffling, rustles and clinks arose as folks returned to their beers and business.

"Seamus, mind giving our friend here a drink? I'm sure he could use it after the day he had." Sierra hunched over the counter, her palms wrapped tightly around a bottle of Jack. He'd expected the same old hostility he'd received yesterday, not the absolute fairness she handled him with, the same way she dealt with her pack. After she'd run out earlier, he'd braced himself for an onslaught of blame. The lack of aggression directed his way disarmed him.

Even though Seamus scowled, he poured a pint of Guinness and passed it over. Dax wrinkled his nose at the foamy dark brew, not being much of a stout man. Still, he wouldn't turn down free beer. Taking the glass with a tilt of his head in the direction of the World's Crankiest Bartender, he swiveled in his seat to face Sierra.

"The amount I'm prepared to drink depends on what your friend Jeremiah figured out with the will." He took a sip from the pint. Even though the beer tasted flat and way too thick, he'd take anything for distraction at this point. His pulse picked up in her presence as her scent wrapped around him—apples and spice.

"He's on his way over to discuss," Sierra responded, her gaze flicking away before she continued. "I…went for a long run earlier." The elephant in the room tap-danced on deafening feet. At some point, they'd have to discuss this mess, but if she wanted to play the avoidance game, he'd already joined the ranks as a professional commitment dodger.

He opened his mouth, ready to deliver a comment about running into his bed, when he froze. This mating bond destroyed his go-to avoidance move, because the second he flirted with her, things got real, fast. Instead of responding, he homed in on the pint in front of him, chugging the murky stout in a couple of gulps before he slid the empty glass back over to Seamus.

"Pretty please?" he asked. Seamus shook his head but acquiesced, filling it with more sludge-like brew. He was in a self-flagellating mood anyway, so the drink helped that punishment along. As he grasped the refilled glass, he scooped his balls off the ground and faced Kanoska again. The mating bond had struck so suddenly he'd forgotten about the previous, painful discovery of the day from hell.

"Rylie happened to fling a revelation in my face," Dax said. If he had a choice in conversations, at least he could broach this one with her. "Pops and the other old folks in the pack might have had such a huge problem with me, because apparently I'm not his blood. Never could explain the blatant favoritism for my brother, but now I'm delivered answers on a silver platter."

Sierra let out a low whistle. "Damn. That's a cold-cock you need time to rebound from," she said, understanding in the brief nod she gave him. To his relief, she didn't paw at him or try to coddle—anything else would've made his skin crawl.

He lifted his pint. "To alcohol. Nature's best therapy," he said, a grin curling his lips. She raised her own bottle in response, those serious eyes glittering as she took another sip. He drank the smooth liquid down, despite the malty, sour taste of it. He let it banish the self-loathing that had taken root in him the second he'd lost control of his pack, the voice in his head sounding too reminiscent of dear old Dad.

Footsteps pounded behind them, but the conversation in the bar didn't halt in the slightest, so Dax swung around to face the lawyer he'd left studying documents earlier.

Jeremiah approached with the manila folder. Those glasses still looked off on the guy wearing a dark-blue work shirt and jeans with more holes than a sieve. He slammed the folder onto the bar and let out a grunt in the process. The man had been a veritable bucket of sunshine so far, all growls and temper—not as if Dax expected more from a wolf.

"So, after scanning over this beastly thing, I've got a mixed bag of news," Jeremiah said with a sigh. In seconds, Seamus slid a gin and tonic in front of the man. They clasped hands, a grin spreading on both of their faces. Dax's stomach wrenched in an ugly way at the reminder of what he used to have—an entire pack of allies he'd grown up with, a family who, even when they fought, stayed together. Until his dad had passed, dragging the pack into chaos.

"Hit me with the worst of it," Dax said, taking another sip from his glass. He had the tolerance of a freight train so he'd have to knock back a keg of these before the effects started hitting him, but as far as distractions went, drinking provided enough of one. Even though Sierra had grown quiet, she had a solid presence that didn't need announcing and while everyone else ran their mouths, she watched and observed. No wonder the woman ran circles around most packs in this region.

"Your father's wishes mean jack shit in both human and shifter terms. The problem with your pack interfering has no backing. Why they chose to interfere is all on them." Jeremiah squeezed the lime into his gin and tonic before taking a sip.

Dax let out a sigh, tugging the brim of his baseball cap. "I think I might have the answer on that one."

Jeremiah's brow quirked before he continued. "Here's the big problem. Since the pack interfered in the alpha fight and your lot can't seem to come to a resolution, that invites the Tribe to step in, and they don't look too kindly on packs who can't manage themselves. Once they arrive, the rights to your land and pack are in flux. Anyone in the region can try to stake their claim."

"So, you're saying my territory will be a free-for-all?" Dax asked, bringing a hand to his temple.

"What if he petitions the Tribe for arbitration, given the first transgression of his pack?" Sierra interrupted, her gaze sharp as a blade. Jeremiah rubbed the stubble on his chin, letting out a sigh. When they'd first met, Dax would've pegged him for a meathead, but after witnessing the man navigate his way through those legal documents and a more serious, less aggressive side, Dax caught the intelligence in his eyes.

"If he's the one petitioning against his brother, he may be able to stall the free-for-all on the land and settle it in a one-on-one fight. They'd need to go through with the fight for dominance, though, and if the Tribe deemed neither a suitable alpha by the end, then the land would revert to whatever shifters could stake the strongest claim," Jeremiah said between sips from his drink. He glanced to Dax. "Sure you want to put your land and pack out there for grabs? We could scoop it up in a heartbeat."

"But we wouldn't," Sierra butted in, right as Dax's skin began to prickle. "Because we made an arrangement, and we'll be true to our word."

He flashed her a smile, trying to ignore the way his gratitude for her traveled deeper to his gut, the feeling more intense than camaraderie for a packmate. "Then that settles it. We're bringing the big, bad Tribe tromping down to our neck of the woods."

"Joy." Jeremiah wrinkled his nose as he slammed back the rest of his gin and tonic. "Let me know when you need more counsel." He met Dax's gaze. "Sounds like you got the raw deal on this one, my man. Sorry to hear."

Dax's brows lifted, understanding not something he'd expected from a man who'd growled at him on first meeting. "Hey, Pops did me the service of weeding out the disloyal members. Maybe we can start fresh and create a better rep for ourselves than an aggressive group of assholes."

"That's one way of testing loyalty," Jeremiah said, sliding his empty glass over to Seamus. He pushed the manila folder over to Dax as he rose from his seat. "If you'll all excuse me, I've got some extra energy to blow off, and Mira's been giving me the eye."

Sierra snorted by his side. "Dream on, brother. She's been giving you the eye because you're a pain in her ass, not because she wants to sleep with you."

He winked as he sauntered over to one of the pool tables, tossing his hand in the air. "We'll see, boss."

Which left the two of them together again, sans buffer. As Jeremiah exited stage left, all the familiar tension they'd grappled with earlier returned. Despite the way he'd been able to avoid the conversation before, he used his revelation card up, and with the way Sierra regarded him, her lips pursed and her dark eyes burning with an unrepentant seriousness, he couldn't avoid the crash course of this conversation.

"So, I shouldn't have run out back there," Sierra said, grabbing the topic by the balls and throwing it right into the open. Not like he expected anything less from their brief interactions. "And don't bother playing coy, because I know you felt it too."

Dax let out a long sigh, running a hand through his hair. A million evasions danced through his head, but the second he tried, she'd slice right through them. Sierra took no-nonsense to a new degree. "Look," he started. "I barely know you."

To his surprise, her shoulders relaxed at his statement. He'd half-expected some fierce argument, some intense fight from her, but they'd both had this surprise strangle them in the middle of what had been a no-strings fling.

She opened her mouth, ready to speak, when the door flew open with a loud smack, one drawing every eye in the room.

Ally raced into the tavern, eyes wide and glowing amber, her claws out. "Dax, they're attacking."

Chapter Seven

Sierra shot from her seat the second the door flew open. Adrenaline coursed through her even before Dax's packmate stepped in. Dax rushed to Ally, galvanized by her words as his muscles moved with the smooth glide of liquid.

"What's Drew doing?" he asked, his voice sharpening.

"Overheard him at the usual bar," she said. "I slipped out before they noticed me, but he's bringing his group around our way and giving us the choice of accepting him as alpha or he'll beat us into submission."

A feral growl ripped from Dax's throat, surprising Sierra. Thus far, the man had shown iron control over his beast, but this tapped a direct vein into protection territory, and as an alpha, protecting his pack was priority number one.

"I'll back you up." The words slipped from her lips before she registered them. Sure, she shouldn't be diving into his problems headfirst, and the mating bond had already started messing with her mind, but she wouldn't stand back and watch while his brother bullied his way into the position. As far as neighbors went, she much preferred Dax. Not just because the man made her hormones rev, but because despite his snarky comments, the man upheld the same sort of moral code she did. That, she could respect.

Finn sidled over to her with a smile. "You better not be leaving me out of a fight, Sierra." She didn't miss the way Dax's gaze slipped to her, those eyes blazing with unbidden possessiveness. She bit back her groan. Wolves were legendarily jealous when mated, and she could guess the feeling transferred to any type of shifter. Already, her skin prickled with how close Ally stood to him. As much as she'd plotted out her avoidance strategy with the mating bond, her body reacted to him, betraying her plans.

"Anyone who feels like blowing off some steam can join in," Sierra announced bar-wide. Aggression rushed through her, the unspent sexual tension from before brimming under the surface and burning fast into irritation. "We're going to pummel some traitors into the ground."

Dax nodded, his face grim. "Avoid killing if possible," he added. "Those who choose to come, thank you. We won't turn down help." He flicked his gaze to her, the slight tilt of his head conveying his unspoken thanks. Dax turned, leading the way out the door with Ally following close behind.

Finn clapped a hand on her shoulder and Raven sidled over from where she'd been playing pool. The petite woman's gaze sparked silver. Apparently, she wasn't the only one jonesing for an outlet. "Let's go," Sierra said, following them out of Beaver's Tavern.

Dax hopped into his truck and Ally swung into the passenger's seat. The blonde leaned in to place a hand on his arm, the contact making Sierra blink back red. Finn tapped her on the shoulder.

"Uh, boss," he said, distracting her for a moment. "You're growling."

Sierra swallowed hard, the realization like a slap to the face. "Just looking forward to pummeling some mountain lion ass into the ground," she said, stalking along the gravel to her beat-up sedan. She slammed the door as she settled into the driver's seat, the control of being behind the wheel doing wonders for her temper. Control was the key cornerstone to her life. and the very reason she had raced out of Dax's house this morning.

Being mated to a stranger had never figured into her plans. She'd have dived in for a casual fling with Dax, a way to burn off aggression, not in a thousand years expecting the mating bond to emerge. The whole thing had spiraled so far out of her control she'd been unable to stave the urge to run, to escape. Yet when Dax had arrived in the bar, she'd swallowed the fears percolating under the surface and grabbed the issue by the throat. He'd see reason, for sure. She peeled across the parking lot, letting the fury riding through her out onto the gravel.

Except reason didn't ride the wheel of the possessiveness that flooded her when another female put her hands on him. The mere idea of him made her thighs clench together. And her wolf had approved the moment the bond emerged, the animal instinct overtaking rational thought.

"Care to share what's going on with our feline friend?" Finn asked. Even though his tone came across as casual, she caught the edge of demand there. Her pack wasn't used to being kept in the dark about much, and besides, her policy of honesty and transparency worked for her and the crew. Problem was, she hadn't even discussed any of this with Dax yet. As much as she spilled most of her dirt to Finn, this existed between her and the Silver Springs alpha, no one else.

"He's got family troubles out the ass. Turns out, his father played favorites, and even though Dax tried to fight for the position of alpha, major members of the pack broke up the match and drove him off, leaving his brother to lead." Even though Finn had been angling for the reason behind her sudden territorial attitude, he'd have to wait on the explanation. Until at least she figured out her next move.

Finn lifted a brow but didn't push. "So, this is a big family feud," he said, allowing her the distraction.

Raven leaned forward from the backseat, her hand resting on the back of the driver's seat. "Heard rumors from Jer that the Tribe might be coming to town?" she asked, hesitation in her tone.

"You heard right," Sierra said, gripping her wheel more tightly as she pumped the gas to soar across the highway. "I called my contact earlier. We've got nothing to hide, so their visit won't concern us in the slightest." Dax's truck zoomed along at top speed, but in her beast of a car, she barely had to try to keep up.

The way Raven lapsed into silence nagged her, but Sierra allowed her friend her quiet. Not like she planned on parading her own problems on Front Street yet.

Finn shrugged, saving the awkward silence that descended. "As long as I get to bash in some skulls, I'm happy. Things have been so quiet on the home front I'm about ready to snore my way through Sunday. What's the point in being pack beta if your alpha is a control freak and navigates us out of most fights?"

"All these cats stomping over our territory has me itching for a fight too," Sierra agreed. "What's say we establish some dominance to sate the restless wolf inside?" Dax's truck swerved to the right, so she followed suit, heading down another winding road farther into backwater towns her kind reigned over in this part of Pennsylvania.

"Sounds like a plan," Raven agreed from the back seat, leaning closer to the front. Sierra glanced back. She didn't miss the way the striking woman stared at Finn, longing clear as day in those soft eyes. Not like her second-in-command had ever given the bartender a similar look or the same sort of devotion. She was in good company for the conflicted.

Up ahead, the truck's brake lights blazed, and Dax made a sharp right down an even narrower road. Gravel crunched under the tires as Sierra kept pace along the small, winding road. At the end, it branched into a circle, surrounded by the lights glowing through the windows of several Cape Cod houses. These places nestled in the middle of the woods like this spelled "hearth and home" in a way that spoke to her—at least,, until she screeched to a stop behind Dax's truck and stepped out of her car.

Screams and growls rent the air, the sort that crawled into her veins, jarring her protective instinct. Drew and his band of assholes must've beaten them here.

Dax took off at a flat run with Ally close behind. Sierra couldn't help the competitive streak working through her veins. Even though her pack wasn't in danger, the wolf inside her snapped at the leash. She transitioned in the blink of an eye, one moment standing on two feet, the next on four as her claws clicked against the gravel. Her clothes drifted in shreds to the ground.

Sierra lunged forward, slicing across the distance in her faster form. She loped across the loamy earth, the blades of grass squishing beneath the pads of her paws. Dax shifted liquid fast into the tawny mountain cat with coiled muscles and a peppering of ash streaks through his pelt. They vaulted for the door, which hung by the hinges, splinters littering the tiled floor inside and sour light from the entryway spilling onto the front porch. The tang of blood already burst in a violent bloom, threading through the heavy air.

A loud hiss came from inside the house.

Dax's gaze flashed as he plunged through the entryway. Sierra skidded to a halt right before diving in after him. Racing headfirst into danger was never a wise move, but his impulse to protect his pack would drown out any precautions. Between her and Dax, one of them had to think clearly. Ally blazed past her, rushing in to back up her alpha. As much as Sierra's heart pumped with adrenaline, pushing her to follow suit, she refused to ignore the tug in her gut telling her otherwise.

A whiff of an unrecognizable scent caught her nose, and she followed the trail, circling around to the back of the house. She navigated with the stealth afforded to her kind, the silent approach of a wolf. Bypassing the vinyl siding, she reached the edge where the yard sprawled, shared by several properties. Sierra stuck to the shadows, ignoring the way her veins jittered with anticipation of a brawl to focus on the hunt instead.

No one stood watch as she'd expected.

Sierra crept to the back, trying to ignore the shouts and yowls coming from inside. The fresh-cut grass overpowered most of the scents around this place, but a hint of something tinny caught her attention. Her snout trailed along the ground as she soaked in the rich loam of the dirt below, the smells causing her nose to tingle. The urge to fight thrummed through her stronger than ever, but it now warred with a sense of wrong, one she couldn't quite place.

Feet away, something metallic glinted in the grass.

Sierra padded forward, each step cautious. The closer she approached, the more the scent filled her nose—metal, decay and something unidentifiable. The moonlight illuminated the object, making her stop still in her path. Pipes bound together with an electric fuse on the end and a timer attached.

This wasn't a negotiation in the slightest. This classified as either outright annihilation or a trap.

Those bastards had brought pipe bombs.

Rage burned fiercely inside Sierra's chest, followed by dread. That thing could explode at any moment while Dax and the others were all inside the house. She nudged the timer with her snout to get a glimpse of the numbers, but without hands, she couldn't move it to the right angle. She doubted any of Drew's men were waiting around in there, not with the literal ticking bomb out back. She shifted into her human form at once, breaking into a run even before she settled on two feet. The grass slipped beneath her bare soles, but she tossed her hands out for balance, not pausing for a moment as she rocketed toward the door.

The couple of steps creaked under her feet as she raced up them before colliding with the door. It gave under her force with no effort, presumably left open by whatever bastard had sneaked out to leave the surprise. Inside, growls lit the air as Dax hunched over in the main room, shifted to two feet as he worked at slicing the bonds of a family who'd been bound, husband, wife and their three kids. Ally had pitched in, but Sierra's wolves were nowhere to be found. Chances were, like her, they'd taken inventory of more immediate concerns. More houses marked this stretch.

"Don't bother untying," Sierra commanded, her voice filling the room. "Get them as far away from this house as possible. There's a pipe bomb out back."

The word itself detonated in the thick air, a serious threat unable to be ignored. Dax's eyes widened, his nostrils flared, but rather than wasting breath responding, he got straight to work. Sierra rushed up and grabbed one of the girls, who couldn't have been older than seven. The little guy by her side had already been untied and his other older sister grabbed his hand.

"Follow me," Sierra said. The little boy looked up to Dax, who nodded in confirmation as he lifted the mother, carrying her across the threshold of the house as they headed for the door. Ally finished sawing through the cord keeping the father bound. Sierra didn't look back, already heading for the door with her precious cargo. Ugly burns wound around the skin where the cord touched, and the second it scraped against her skin, the area sizzled where a residue imprinted. *Bastards must've coated the cord in colloidal silver and bound them while wearing gloves.*

Anger ripped through her in a wildfire blaze that they'd threaten this family, that they'd torture and try to kill children. That the cowards would defy the Tribe rules of fighting by the claw and fang. Guns and bombs were human weapons, dishonorable to shifter-kind.

She burst out the front door with the children. Based on the way the pipe bomb pricked her nostrils, the explosive was ready to blow.

"Keep running until you reach the cars," she urged, giving the oldest kid a push. The girl tugged on her little brother's hand, guiding him forward to keep running on their own. Sierra's claws flashed out quick as she snipped the final cords binding the girl in her arms and set the kid down before nodding ahead. Once the patter of feet sounded behind her, she whipped around.

Right in time to see the house explode into flames.

Chapter Eight

Dax had just risen to his feet when a blast of heat rolled his way. Light sparked in his eyes when he turned toward the house, the blinding gusts rolling out of it spelling seven shades of destruction. Rage ignited his veins and scorched his soul at witnessing the destruction Drew had caused to his own people, the family and friends he'd grown up with. He scanned for his packmates. Sierra had staggered far enough away while the kids sprinted past him as fast as their short legs could carry them. *Safe.*

Ally and Rick raced away from the house, but not fast enough.

Flames gusted behind them, the black, oily smoke pouring into the sky in torrents. Dax's throat squeezed tight. All this destruction because he'd challenged his brother for the role of alpha. Now, his people suffered.

"I'm going to check the other houses," Sierra said, emanating calm despite the chaos raging around them. Her gaze glowed amber, and with fluid agility, she transformed into wolf form before launching off. Gratitude pounded a heavy beat in Dax's chest for her level head and for her strength. After witnessing her competence in action, he trusted her to protect his pack.

He hurtled toward Ally, who'd stumbled to the ground. Rick thrashed around, trying to extinguish the flames threatening to devour his skin. Ally's brows drew together, her teeth gritted in pain as she pushed herself up. She leaned on her left leg, the right one hanging limp with a streak of the colloidal silver from Rick's bonds melted there. A long, jagged wound ran down her calf, blood rushing at an alarming rate.

"Marcy," Dax called out, "hand over a piece of cloth. Anything."

Marcy kicked leaves as she rushed over, the brunette ripping a section of her camisole off and passing the fabric his way. A second later, her knees slammed to the ground next to her husband. Tears streamed down her face, but the woman took firm action, stomping out the residual flames. Dax knelt by Ally's side, taking the rag and wrapping it tightly around the gushing wound on her calf. Already sweat beaded on her brow, and she swayed where she stood, the shock settling in. With the colloidal silver impeding quick healing, this would leave an ugly scar.

"Can you make it to the car?" he asked. She nodded, her fierce gaze steady, despite the pain. "That's my girl." He squeezed her shoulder before stepping away. If his brother was tying up his people and planting bombs, this wouldn't be the only house under siege. This neighborhood was one of the largest clusters of his pack, one his brother had targeted without mercy. In the distance, a wolf's fur shone under the moonlight, running with those long, loping strides that marked her apart. Sierra headed for the cabin on the far right.

A couple of other packmates sprinted from their houses, followed by the wolves Sierra had brought with her. They rushed as fast as possible towards the unpaved circle that constituted a road out here where their cars waited. The pop and crackle of Marcy and Rick's house filtered into his hearing, the sound jolting the adrenaline in his veins. He shifted, hitting the ground on all fours and taking off at the sort of run to make the breeze ruffle through his fur. His brother would pay for this. Causing him problems was one thing. Hell, attacking him, fine. But taking out this split on their people?

Unforgiveable.

His paws pounded against the ground with the increasing crescendo of a war drum, the sound thrumming in his ears. Despite the chaos that reigned, Drew and the elders of Silver Spring were nowhere in sight. Dax tuned out the shouts, cries and the sight of his packmates fleeing their houses, before following Sierra to the house on the far right. Lana and her husband, Greg, lived in that house, and his brother never would've let those tough fighters alone.

Sierra prowled around the back of the house as he neared. She lifted her head, catching his gaze. He dipped his head in acknowledgment—she'd investigate for a bomb while he went to release anyone inside. In the distance, a boom quaked the air, the sort to make his fur stand on edge. He couldn't look, not yet. If he caught sight of the destruction, he'd be pulled toward the chaos, beyond the logic of doing what he could to save whoever waited inside here.

He rammed into the door, and it flew back to slap against the wall, left ajar by whoever had intruded.

The second he stepped in, he wished he hadn't. Sobs echoed through the house, soul-destroying ones, the sort signaling the worst sort of devastation had already descended. His stomach clenched as he approached, padding past the overturned benches in the foyer, a bent lamp, and the shattered glass of broken picture frames. The sound carried from the kitchen. He peered around the corner, his muscles tensed and ready for action. However, only one person sat tied to a chair in the middle of the room.

Lana's hands gripped tightly around the edges of her chair. She was unable to shift due to those cords applied with colloidal silver. Greg lay sprawled on the floor, unmoving. Dax leaped to his best friend, sniffing around the body. Blood pooled, the scent pungent. Greg didn't blink, didn't twitch, and even this close, Dax couldn't hear the distant pulse of a heartbeat and didn't spot the slow rise and fall of breathing. Cold doused him like ice water.

He'd grown up with them, run through the woods by their side as they learned to control the shift, as they trained together under the elders. Greg and Lana had been smitten since they were kids, the fated type of romance most of the pack longed for. He'd been the gruff sort, but her joyful spirit coaxed him out and softened his edges every time. Now, Greg wouldn't smile again. Wouldn't scrap with Dax when the rage burned fierce or run a late-night diner trip to stave off their inevitable hangovers.

Dax shifted to two feet, barely aware of his surroundings as he walked over to the kitchen drawer and tugged the metal handle to pull out a knife. Lana didn't pay attention to him, tears coming too fast and furious to notice. He sliced through the bonds, and those hateful cords collapsed to the ground. Without the silver-soaked tethers holding her in place, Lana sagged, careening to the kitchen floor.

He knelt in front before she could hit the ground, and instead, she collapsed against his chest. Dax wrapped his arms around her, the wetness from her tears imprinting on his skin. The door creaked, drawing his attention up.

Sierra stepped into view, already shifted back to human form. Her brows furrowed, a line creasing between them at the sight she witnessed. "No bomb out back. Didn't realize they'd already achieved maximum damage in here."

Even as he held Lana in his arms, his rage numbed to shock that his brother would've gone this far to grasp power. Someone rested a hand on his shoulder. He looked to Sierra, whose dark eyes shone with empathy.

"I'll carry her over," she volunteered. "Dax, your people need you right now. Many of them are gathered in the parking lot, watching the blaze steal their homes. They need their alpha. If your people require safe haven, Red Rock will open our borders."

His heart strained in his chest. She'd been steady as stone, an equal in every way throughout this entire nightmare. He hadn't questioned she'd watch his back as they'd dove into the flames together. And when he needed it most, as his childhood friend lay dead on the floor, she reminded him of the duty he'd fought for. Of why these individuals had been targeted in the first place. The worst thing he could do for them now was cower or indulge in his grief. He had to rise up and prove they'd made the right choice, despite the heavy cost.

She placed her arms around Lana's shoulders from behind as he rose to his feet. "I'll meet you out there, alpha."

Even though grief threatened to tear him to pieces and even though every step away from Greg's body haunted him anew, Dax made his way to the door. He broke into a flat run the second he stepped outside. The mountain lion within begged to come out, to race and roar, but he remained on both feet, needing to stay levelheaded. His lion would drag him to claim vengeance against his brother after the destruction wrought here tonight.

Thinking with the wild side, with his heart and not his head, was what had gotten him into this mess in the first place. It was what had brought him to Sierra Kanoska's doorstep searching for help. The cool head she kept even amid the worst rage – that was the sort of alpha a pack respected. The sort they needed right now. And that was what Dax Williams would be.

The ground changed from the soft squish of earth to the flat roughness of gravel as he sprinted along to his truck. After shifting to two feet first, he nabbed his spare clothes from inside. Dax tossed them on and zipped his jeans as the pack gathered around him.

Their footsteps echoed and their gazes pressed into him, the tension in the air so thick he could taste the grief. The loss. The rage. He rolled his shoulders, letting the intensity of their emotions rush through him. They surrounded him here, but beyond, flames licked the cabins, the incendiary glow striking a similar spark inside him from the injustice they'd faced tonight.

"Men and woman of the Silver Springs pack." His voice boomed through the lot, drowning out the distant crackle of their homes. "Tonight, we have suffered at the hands of those we considered our brothers and sisters. Those who we grew up alongside, who we believed could never betray us."

Sierra approached from the distant house with Lana in tow as the woman sagged against the alpha. His people continued to gather closer and closer to his side while he spoke, capturing their attention. Even though his heart stretched like frayed rope, he sucked in a deep breath and continued.

"Drew ordered this attack on the very people he once wished to govern, but that is the furthest from what an alpha does. An alpha protects his own. We respect the rules passed down to us from the Tribe, passed on from the great spirits of the animals we shift into. We settle our disputes honorably with claw and fang. Never with pipe bombs set outside the houses of families, and never to harm our innocent and young."

Marcy's eyes shone with tears and she ran her hands through Rick's fur. He'd shifted into his cat form to further his healing, but the burns created vivid ragged spots where the fur had scorched off.

"We won't sit idle." His voice grew deep and dark with the raw anguish of what they suffered. "We've called the Tribe in, and I'll make Drew face me fairly in a battle for our land. I'll beat him, and we will reclaim our lands so the Silver Springs pack is no longer severed in two. My people, we will fight to keep our homes, because you—you are loyal and you are strong. United, we won't let this horror go unpunished. We will prevail."

He lapsed into silence as the energy sapped out of him, poured into every word he spoke. Glistening eyes and somber faces surrounded him, but as his shoulders relaxed and his mouth closed, his pack reacted. One by one, their growls lit the air, their cries a mournful cacophony taken to the stars. Sierra lifted her chin and howled, even in her human form, the sound piercing and eerie enough to prickle his arms. Everyone surrounding him rumbled with rage and grief, responding as one pack, the Silver Springs he was so honored to be a part of. The pack he was determined to lead until his dying day, no matter what the fates spelled out for him.

"In the morning, we will begin to clear the rubble and figure out a way to proceed. As it stands, we have packmates sustaining serious injuries. Help who you can into cars and let's get them to safety." The second the words left his lips, his pack launched into motion. Ignitions turned, bringing car engines to life, and shifters in human or lion form piled into trucks, sedans, whatever possible. Ally curled in her mountain lion form in the bed of his truck.

Sierra approached with Lana, her arm around the woman's shoulder. "Here's your girl. I've got to grab my people, but my lands are open for any of your pack."

Dax met her gaze and held it for a moment, wishing he could communicate the depth of admiration welling inside him at how she'd stepped up tonight. At how she'd inspired him, keeping him strong when he'd come close to crumbling. He'd never met a more remarkable woman.

He clapped a hand on Sierra's shoulder. He wrapped his other arm around Lana, who slumped against him, numbed from shock. "Thank you. Truly."

She flashed him a grim smile and offered a salute before racing toward her packmates waiting by the car. Dax tightened his grip around Lana as he began trekking to his own. He had a long night ahead of him.

* * * *

Dax turned the knob to his place, and his shoulders sagged as he stumbled in through the door. Already, the thin air of predawn descended, and he'd expended so much energy tonight he wanted to sink into his couch and go comatose. Once he sauntered in through the main room, a familiar scent pricked his nose, drawing his attention.

"If you've come to fight me, plunge a knife in my back and get it over with. I'm fucking exhausted," he called out, too tired to bother with sneaking around or subtlety. He'd lost the capacity for that earlier in the night when his pack had been bombed in their own homes. A creak sounded, followed by slow footsteps in his direction. Dax braced himself for a fight even though every muscle in his body screamed for rest.

"No need to embarrass yourself, kitty cat." Sierra's voice echoed through the corridor as she emerged, those gorgeous hips swinging from side to side.

Dax lifted a brow and crossed his arms. "Funny, I don't remember handing you the key to my place."

Sierra snorted. "Not my fault you left your window unlocked. Didn't even need to bust up your locks." She pulled a bottle of Jack from behind her, the amber liquid sloshing around. "Thought you might need a drink tonight. I've weathered my fair share of rough calls."

Even with the scratches on her cheek, her skin glowed with freshness, and between her shower-wet hair pulled into a ponytail and the lingering scent of soap, she'd clearly seized the chance to clean up. She was the sort of gorgeous that made him salivate, though given how much he reeked, right now he shouldn't be in the same county let alone the same room as her.

Dax accepted the offering of Jack and unscrewed the cap while they walked toward his couch. He caught a whiff of the campfire smell radiating from his shirt and tugged it over his head. The fabric hit the floor with a soft whump.

Sierra settled into the couch as if she belonged there. "Hey, now, no one said this was a booty call."

A lazy smile reached his lips. "The mere sight of me shirtless takes your mind there? Good to know. I'd rather a solid fuck than getting my kumbayas out."

She snorted before bursting into a full laugh, the deep throatiness of her voice sexier than any subtle flirting. "Please, I hear enough bitching from every member of my pack. What makes you think I want to add your whining to the list? I come offering a drink. That's all."

The seriousness in her eyes communicated what she didn't say. The weight of a day like this and the burden of leading a pack could break even the toughest soldier. That she understood the loneliness of lying alone in the dark, consumed by all that noxious guilt. The fact she was willing to stay by his side right now with no expectations or demands offered a comfort he hadn't realized he'd been missing. He'd been coming home to an empty house for so long he'd forgotten the relief of walking in the door and having someone notice he'd been gone. *Having someone care.*

He took a swig of Jack, relishing the burn as the amber fluid rolled down his throat. She snatched the bottle out of his hands and gulped down more. As she rested the bottle on her thigh, the liquid glistened on those sinful lips. Even though he wanted to talk about anything other than what had happened, the events dominated his mind.

She gave him the side-eye. "Since I've had enough of your mouth for the next decade, let's drink with a movie on. We could use the distraction."

Dax shook his head, unable to help his weary smile as he settled back into his couch and grabbed the remote. "Were you just born bossy? Did you slide out of the womb making demands at the doctor?"

"If you've got a natural talent for something, why quash it?" She shrugged, even though her eyes gleamed with wickedness. Dax let out a bark of a laugh. Already the whiskey quelled the fraying edges of his nerves, and while exhaustion squeezed his muscles like pulp, he managed to turn on his TV to a random channel, the flickering images barely registering.

He reached for the bottle, his hand brushing against Sierra's in the process. Even the simple touch jolted him, a shock of electricity he wasn't prepared for. That must come with the whole mate package. The thought stirred the buzzing hornet's nest in his mind, so he took another sip of whiskey and leaned back. Sierra carved her own stretch of space on the opposite side, her legs wide open and her arms lining the back of the couch. The sight sent his blood flow south, even though his body had long since given up on movement.

Despite the stubbornness Sierra wielded like a weapon, after a couple of minutes, her lashes started flickering. Moments later, she sank into the curve of the couch, her head lolling to the side as she conked out. A smirk lifted his lips as he pushed himself up to grab a blanket. He covered her, the amber scent and heat of her teasing him with the not-so-distant memories of the way she'd felt in his arms. Of the taste of those lips.

Dax plunked down on the couch and leaned against the arm, the heavy tug of exhaustion drawing him in like an eddying tide. He placed the bottle on the floor and snagged some of the woolen blanket as he settled in. Might not be the most comfortable sleep, but here would be a hell of a lot better than settling into his dark, empty bed. Here there was whiskey, warmth and a woman who had proved to be extraordinary.

With the threat of the mating bond looming over him, he should be pushing her away and running as far and fast as possible. Yet she'd arrived and offered comfort when no one else had. She'd supported him and given him strength at his weakest.

The more he got to know Sierra Kanoska, the closer to an unavoidable collision he came. She wasn't some casual fling. If he dared fall for her, and if the bond between them deepened any more, he'd find himself mated for life.

Chapter Nine

Sierra's legs creaked as she swung them over the side of the couch. Passing out at Dax's place hadn't been part of the plan, but after the long day she'd had, the comfort of whiskey and warmth in his cabin had lulled her to sleep. She stretched her arms over her head, glancing to the side where Dax slept, his well-defined chest rising and falling with his luscious tanned skin on clear display. He'd curled on the opposite side of the couch rather than in his bed, though she had no idea when he'd hit the hay.

She wrinkled her nose as she hopped off the couch. Time to duck out before he woke up. Whatever audacity had possessed her to show up at his house yesterday sure as hell hadn't lingered.

The normal early light trickled through the window, a regular sight from her sunrise wake-up times. An alpha's work never ended, and she liked to get a head start on the off chance she could field problems before they started. Not like they'd ever dealt with the magnitude of what had happened to the Silver Springs pack last night. After the grief etched on Dax's face at witnessing his people hurt and finding his friend murdered, she couldn't leave him to confront those troubles on his own. Even if this closeness caused the tug toward him to grow all the stronger.

She grabbed her canvas bag off the floor and stood, smoothing out the wrinkles on her pants. Sierra needed to head to her own pack. She'd called her contact in the Tribe yesterday, which meant depending on where the members were along the coast and how many cases they had in their workload, someone could arrive today or tomorrow.

"That would make this the second time you're rushing away from my place." Dax's voice came from behind her. "Am I your dirty secret, Kanoska?" She turned to face him, annoyance thrumming through her chest at his teasing tone. He sat up from the couch, one arm resting on the back while his blue eyes glittered with amusement. Even though his ash-brown hair had the mussed quality of having just woken up, his gaze sharpened to alert, as if he'd been awake the past half hour.

"Obviously," she retorted. "I can't be going back smelling like cat. My wolves will get all riled up."

"Not like I marked you, sweetheart. Though if you want to give them something to talk about, I'd be happy to oblige." At the mention of marking, his tongue darted over his lips and his tone heated. Sierra couldn't help the flush racing through her. Her core sparked to life at the thought of his teeth scraping against her skin and the way those strong hands had caressed her body yesterday.

"Ass. Unlike you cat shifters who lounge around all day, I've got work to do." She crossed her arms, hoping he couldn't scent how her body responded to him. The way his grin widened at her statement hinted he had.

"Let me make you a cup of coffee at least," he said, rolling to his feet with fluid grace before he strode to his kitchen. "Least I can do for the visit last night." He stopped at the doorframe, his hand resting there as his lips pressed together and his gaze turned solemn for once. "Thank you."

The gravity of the words hit her like a sucker punch, a gasp of seriousness from the man who mastered distraction and avoidance. Sierra squeezed the strap of her pack. At that, he ducked into his kitchen, and within seconds, the coffeemaker's hiss resounded through the air. The fragrant scent of freshly brewing coffee wafted over from the kitchen, stilling her feet. As much as she wanted to leave, the lure of coffee was a siren's song she could never conquer.

She wandered in and was rewarded by the sight of Dax's tanned muscles in action as he reached to the top shelf of his cabinet to pull two mugs down.

"The Tribe's been alerted," she offered, hoping to break the awkwardness in the room at the subject they both avoided. The mating bond seemed trivial in comparison to the loss and destruction that had occurred last night.

"Good," he said, grabbing the carafe and pouring the molten liquid into the cups. "Called in the enforcers to report the ruckus so the local cops weren't roped onto the scene. Not like humans want to be roaming around well-known shifter territory. I'm guessing your rise to alpha wasn't this dramatic?" He passed her a mug and nudged the creamer and sugar forward along the countertop. Sierra fixed up her coffee and wrapped her palms around the hot ceramic.

Sierra snorted. "Hell no. My alpha had trained me and a couple of others for a while, so when the time came and he passed, the strongest of the pack got together and duked it out. Everyone had been placing their bets on Finn—he's tough, capable and has a bucketload of charisma. They forgot not only am I smarter, but I'm way more stubborn."

A smirk tugged his lips. "Color me surprised." He leaned against the counter, his snug jeans drawing her eyes to the way they slung low on his hips, a sprinkle of hair following the well-defined trail of his abs. "Mine's turned into the shitshow I'd give my left nut to avoid. Never expected Drew to stoop as low as he did last night though."

"It was some sort of fucked up," she agreed, tension percolating through her with the intensity of the coffee she drank. Sierra raised her lips to the mug and took the first couple of sips.

Dax ran a hand through his hair. "You know I've reached a whole new hellscape when the conversation we left behind last night is a lighthearted distraction. You were about to say something about this mating bond business before Ally burst in with the news?"

The subject switch gave her whiplash, and she ducked her head to blow the steam off her coffee, finding the surface fascinating all of a sudden. Accepting responsibility, leading her people—those actions came readily for her, but the complex burst of emotions surfacing around Dax Williams had turned into a different beast. She could pretend she didn't feel the fire burning inside every time her mind wandered to him or the easy way she enjoyed his company, a comfort she hadn't felt in a long time.

Except Sierra didn't waste time with self-deception. Whatever existed between them was as tangible and real as the bond she'd breached. And the more time they spent together, the deeper she might fall.

She set her cup of coffee on the counter. No point in avoiding the subject. "Why don't we put aside the fact we've got a mating bond? It's a big noose neither of us wants to deal with, so we should proceed like we would if it wasn't there. At the end of the day, if you drive me so nuts I want to run you over with your own stupid truck, the mating bond doesn't make a bit of difference, so let's not give the thing more power than it deserves."

Dax's grin widened, his eyes twinkling with mischief. Sierra's stomach flip-flopped. She had the feeling whatever came out of his mouth next would have her wanting to deck him.

"You know, if the bond hadn't interrupted us, I would've had you pinned against the wall or maybe bent over my couch." His words came out in a purr that stoked her coals into a blaze. Sex oozed from his pores, making it hard to forget the sparks that flew between them the last time they'd crashed together. She lifted her mug again to drink the smooth liquid, the piping-hot coffee not the only reason heat coiled in her belly.

"Glad to see your one-track mind is functioning as normal again," she muttered, trying to ignore the way her body responded to the sound of his voice and the fire in his eyes. The room charged between them, tension descending as if it had never left. After the events of last night, the two of them could use a chance to unwind. Sierra let out a sigh and placed the mug of coffee down. Bad, bad idea. Hopping in the sack with him, however tempting the tango, wouldn't solve any of the problems on the table.

Her phone buzzed in her pocket and she jumped for the distraction, tugging it out. Finn's name blinked onto the screen, so she answered the phone, aware of the way Dax stared at her. Those predatory eyes were the intense sort of gorgeous she couldn't ignore.

"What's happening, Finn?" she asked. Dax's brow rose, and he walked over to grab the cup she'd left on the countertop. Except then he didn't budge, standing inches away with a slight smile on his lips. Sierra glowered at him, knowing what predatory power games he played. She'd been possessed by the same streak of jealousy yesterday, part of the frenzy the mating bond inspired.

"We've got some visitors at the bar, and they're looking for the alpha who summoned them," he said, his tone sharper than normal. Couldn't be anyone but the Tribe to inspire cautiousness from her beta. Multiple people surprised her though, same as their next-day arrival. They must've been dealing with bigger problems in the area than this alpha feud.

"I'm heading out now," she responded, wishing she'd been there to prepare.

"Let Williams know? They're here asking about the Silver Springs pack, figure he'd want to be in on this," Finn replied. Sierra glanced at the looming presence beside her, a faint smile lingering on his lips since the bastard heard every word Finn said.

"Uh, yeah. I'll let him know," Sierra said before hanging up. The second she slipped her phone in her pocket, she glanced up to speak to Dax—only to find him vanished from the spot.

"Going to take a shower before we go," he called as he strode to the bathroom. She balled her hands into fists, following him. If the Tribe was already waiting at her bar, she didn't have time for him to primp and preen. She had to head out now. Sierra clutched the frame of the bathroom door, taking the first step onto the ceramic tiles.

Only to get an eyeful of Dax stripped to nothing again. He turned on the shower, and the spray hissed out. Water streamed down, and he hopped in, leaving the curtain open. Not like the man gave a damn who saw him, and with a body that fine, she didn't blame him.

"Instead of standing there gawking at me, you're welcome to join," he said while he started scrubbing away.

Sierra sucked in a breath, restraining the urge to deck him. "I've got to get to the bar."

"And I'll be two seconds," he responded. "Beaver Tavern won't burn down without you there. Finn seems capable enough to keep them entertained."

"Shocking. With the way you were all up in my business the second he called, I thought you hated his guts." Sierra crossed her arms, refusing to admit how much the sight of Dax in the shower worked for her in a real way right now.

He ducked under the spray to wash the remaining suds off his body before responding. "Can't help it, babe. You make me burn," he said, flashing her a grin as he stepped out, leaving puddles on the tile in his wake. Beads of water glistened on his skin, and the urge rose in Sierra to lick them off his chest and keep heading downward. "But also this bond business messes with my head. I'm not normally the jealous type."

Sierra nodded as she met his gaze. He wasn't the only one experiencing irrational impulses at the moment. "Fine, toss on some clothes, uncivilized one. Let's get out of here." She turned away from him and headed out of the bathroom before she did something stupid. As she glanced back, the feline grin on his face got her blood thumping.

She stepped into the kitchen and poured herself another cup of coffee before slamming the elixir down while Dax rustled in his room to get dressed. Lust didn't bother her. Sierra had screwed around with plenty of guys before. What annoyed her to no end, what drove her absolutely crazy about Dax was that the more she got to know him, the more she liked the man. She shouldered the weight of leadership with no complaints, but she had to admit she enjoyed having someone around who didn't fall under her rule, someone who understood.

Dax emerged from his room. His shorter strands had already dried under the brim of his Flyers cap, and his undershirt glued to his shower-damp chest. Even in simple jeans and a T-shirt, he emanated the raw power of an alpha with the dangerous gaze of a mountain lion. "Mind if I hitch a ride?"

Sierra's brow rose. "This some flimsy ploy to spend more time with me?"

His grin widened. "Or maybe I want the chance to get you back to my place tonight."

Sierra rolled her eyes as she walked out of his door, the urge to get going returning full-force. She loped over to her beat-up car parked off to the side and grabbed the door handle. Dax locked up and stood in the center of his driveway, arms crossed and his brow lifted with the question still hanging in the air.

She heaved a sigh and tapped the top of her car. "Stop wasting time and hop in, jackass."

Dax slipped over faster than she could blink and slunk into the passenger seat as she opened her own door. He wrapped his broad arm around the driver's seat as he leaned forward. "Hurry up, Sierra," he teased, his gaze twinkling. "We've got somewhere to be." She plunked into the driver's seat and gripped the steering wheel so hard she nearly tore it off. As she turned on the car and began to edge out of his driveway, Dax continued, "You're growling, babe. Might not want to show up to meet the Tribe brimming with aggression."

Sierra forced a smile as the car rumbled down the gravel, and she emerged past the forest into the sun-splattered asphalt of the highway. "Well, you've earned your place as the most singularly annoying individual I've ever met."

"At least I stand out from the crowd," he replied with a smart grin. As much as he made her skin prickle with irritation, relief spread in her chest at the way he cracked jokes with her, the same charming, teasing man she met a couple of days ago. Yesterday had been the intense sort of day to break anyone, but he'd proved himself man enough to step up to the plate and resilient enough to not let his brother's crimes destroy him.

Sierra's car flew across the highway, the tall pines from the neighboring forests flickering by. Fresh air danced through the open windows, the acute aroma of ozone mixing with Dax's cedar musk. When they first met, the foreign scent of the mountain lion brushed her wolf's fur the wrong way, but too fast it had become familiar. Now her wolf stirred for him in a different way, the animal side of her able to bond much faster than the human. After all, Sierra might take people on their honor and might give them a chance, but she didn't trust easily.

The guys she'd bothered trusting always left, so why try? She had the pack by her side, a group of people she could depend on and that filled the void for her. Sierra swallowed, her tongue sticking to the roof of her mouth. At least, it had filled the void. The more time she spent around Dax, the more the ache grew in her chest, the desperate longing for an equal to spend her years with. And that terrified her more than anything, because as soon as she dove in, as soon as she let down her defenses and allowed the vulnerability she protected in a fierce way to poke through, he would leave. They always left.

Dax lapsed into a silence she didn't trust, his gaze flicking her way like a brand as his fingertips danced along the edge of the rolled-down window. Beaver Tavern stood out at the end of the street, the cream exterior accented by oak and the surrounding trees providing a haven she always took comfort in. Her tires screeched as she braked and pulled into a parking spot. A couple of trucks and SUVs she didn't recognize took up spots, and this early they were the only other vehicles in the lot, since the bar didn't open for another hour.

"Ready to go meet the Tribe?" she asked, her hand resting on the gearshift.

Dax ran his hand through his hair as he forced a smile. "What can go wrong? My brother's already set about torturing and murdering my packmates. In the wake of that, a couple of heavyweights from the Tribe are nothing."

Sierra shrugged as she stepped out of her car. "Dax?" she said, meeting his eyes as they faced each other on the opposite sides of her car, her arms resting on the top. "You've got the high ground on this. You're the rightful alpha of the Silver Springs, and you will claim your pack." The ire in her voice reflected the way the injustice he'd experienced affected her.

Sierra lifted her chin and set off in the direction of the tavern. Dax slipped beside her, his palm resting on her shoulder. He dipped forward, his lips brushing her cheek. The touch set her nerves ablaze, the quick burst of a flare inside her.

"Thanks," he whispered in her ear, the heat of his breath tickling her and making her hyperaware of how close he stood. Sierra bit her lip and nodded before she gave in to the impulse to jump his bones. Her hands balled into fists as she quickened her pace.

The most dangerous shifters on the East Coast didn't frighten her in the slightest compared to the mountain-lion menace by the name of Dax Williams.

Chapter Ten

Well, Dax had wanted distraction, but he didn't think meeting the infamous Tribe with a raging hard-on could be considered putting his best foot forward. No matter how he tried to focus, the bloom of Sierra's arousal in the air wasn't helping tamp his intense lust. He sucked in a deep breath and focused on nasty-ass things like wrinkled, paper-thin skin, the moldy can of tomatoes he had in the fridge and the bottle of Midori he'd killed as a teen, turning his puke neon green for an entire day. By the time she opened the bar door, he was ready to face the big beaters who waited inside.

Dax stepped in, the foreign scent hitting him full force. Sure, the stench of wet dog clung to this place like plaster, but the presence of the Tribe brought the sort of power that made his nose tingle. These were the strongest of their kind, imbued with one of the animal spirits that shifters were descended from. Shamans had created his kind as warriors back when the magic users existed en masse. Now, the few remaining only poked their heads out of their remote hovels and communes to anoint new Tribe members.

Dax walked forward, shoulders back and head high. Against the brawn these folks touted, he had to have machismo firing on all cylinders if he hoped to compete. With his position as alpha as shaky as a drunk at Christmas, he was already knee-capped.

"I assume you're the alpha of the Red Rock pack?" a woman's voice called from the opposite side of the tavern. Sierra nodded, taking the lead as they wound their way over to the round table where five vicious-looking bastards sat. Even though Sierra's expression had turned to granite, he could feel the tension buzzing off her the same way it emanated from him.

Their footsteps echoed through the quiet bar as they approached the Tribe members who'd arrived. Finn manned the taps, pouring pints for the visitors with a frown on his face as he watched them warily. The woman who spoke stood, though the others remained seated—not like that diminished the sheer power rolling off them. Even though she couldn't be taller than five feet, her short stature did little to diminish her lethality. Every inch of cocoa skin her tank top and shorts revealed was corded muscle.

Two big guys promised to compete with him and Finn for brawniest, the sort of men who would tower once they stood to full height. Another of the women had a lean, lanky frame, far from willowy since every spare inch of her packed swimmer's muscle. A shorter, stockier guy had a scowl like a bulldog and a pockmarked mug to boot.

What would make anyone blink twice were the intricate tribal tattoos coiling across their arms and trailing down their legs. The shamans used them to bind the great spirits of the shifters to these individuals, which created the source of their abilities. Shifters had an advantage over humans with the way they could transform, but those chosen by the spirits were blessed with enhanced speed, strength and elemental abilities to set them apart from the rest. Only fair that by accepting the spirit, they were bound to the service of shifter-kind, small forces throughout the continents who maintained peace and resolved conflicts with honor, morality and justice.

"And you're the one petitioning for alpha of the Silver Springs pack?" The short chick fixed her gaze on him, her eyes glowing silver. The air crackled and popped between them, the challenge clear in her statement.

Dax gave her with a level look. "I am the rightful alpha of Silver Springs. I'm petitioning for my pack's land to be returned from the hands of a traitor who tore us apart and slaughtered defenseless members of Silver Springs. Who threatened our young." He delivered his words with tempered rage, cooled and hardened from last night into something concrete. Something defining.

One of the brawny guys smirked, causing some of the seriousness to deflate from the room. "Just trying to assess the situation."

Sierra pulled over chairs with a squeak and they joined the Tribe members at the table. Within minutes, Finn swung by with pints of the amber lager they had on tap, making a couple of rounds until he filled the table. He grabbed a seat himself, flipping the chair backward and leaning over to listen. Dax palmed the cold glass, which pressed against his hand like a sedative.

The sheer presence of the Tribe had his lion pacing and growling within, a kick to the chest that sped up by the minute.

The short chick took a sip of beer before placing the glass on the table with a loud clink. "Name's Navi. Let's stop dicking around, and get to the brass tacks of why you dragged us into your family mess."

Dax lifted an eyebrow. "Don't know—seems to me with how quick you lot arrived, all your busy Tribe work must be on the slow side."

The slender woman placed a hand on the shoulder of the muscular guy beside her, who'd begun growling. "Knock it off, Akio." She thwacked the guy. "You can thank Sierra for filling me in on the situation. We've been friends for a long time, and I respect her enough that if she says this is an issue, I believe her. Besides, we happened to be in the area. We had other business in the region."

"Thanks again, Jess." Sierra lifted her pint in appreciation and a slow smile curled her lips. The Red Rock alpha was full of surprises. "Last night his brother and the other section of the pack attacked Dax's people and the bastards used pipe bombs. Do you mind looking into that?"

Jess's brows furrowed as she exchanged a glance with Akio before resting her gaze on Dax. "Pipe bombs? And you can place your brother at the scene of the crime with a witness?" Even though Navi's mouth twisted with a dark scowl, she didn't offer more information. The whole lot of them remained tight-lipped.

Dax let out a frustrated sigh, tugging the brim of his cap. While he might be able to pin other folks in the pack, he hadn't caught sight or scent of his brother last night.

Navi pounded her fist on the table to get attention, the thump drawing every eye. They all snapped to alert. The Tribe member brimmed with power, but patience wasn't a strong suit. "That matter will be dealt with at once. After we finish assessing the scene of yesterday's crime, we'll gauge whether Drew can contest for alpha of your pack and territory. Hearsay doesn't count as testimony, and you have to admit, your personal reasons for blaming the attack on him hold bias."

Dax gritted his teeth, forcing back a growl at his disapproval. Sierra shot him daggers, her gaze burning into him. He sucked in a deep breath, regaining his composure before speaking. "Then level with me. What do I need to do to claim official leadership of my pack?"

Navi let out a hissed breath through her clenched teeth. "Your pack's already made a mess of that. Most folks manage to govern on their own, obeying the rules of a fair fight for dominance to decide who's next to lead. Yours, however, drove you out."

Dax's stomach sank at the way they regarded him—he recognized the look, since he'd garnered it a lot growing up. *Pity*. Pity for the boy who was never in his father's good graces, even though he'd never had a clue why until now. Familiar irritation swelled like the tide, the anger that folks refused to look at him for what he could do, only who had spurned him.

Jess sighed, running a hand through her copper curls. "Since your pack can't be trusted to govern fairly, we step in. Your pack and territory becomes contested—open to challenge for any shifter group in the region who wants to claim them. Not only will you have to fight and defeat your brother if he's not tied to last night, but anyone else who has their eye on the area. If you or your brother win, the Silver Springs pack will remain as is. However, if one of the other local shifter packs takes over, they'll receive your land and the Silver Springs pack will be dissolved, the members sent to the closest mountain lion packs."

Dax held back his sigh, not betraying an inch of the disappointment that raged through him. After the injuries his pack had suffered last night, he wanted to end their agony. He owed them a place to live in peace and as a united pack, since it had all gotten splintered in the wake of his father's death. Dax had hoped to avoid their lands becoming contested, but if that was what it took to reunite his pack and have a fair fight for alpha, then he'd take the chance.

"They can remain on my land while you're going through these trials," Sierra offered. He glanced over at her and saw understanding in her sable gaze. The look soothed him like a balm to his nerves, and their deep, powerful connection flushed him with gratitude.

The other big Latino guy spoke, his voice a motor's rumble. "Don't listen to Jareth's dramatics. You won't be fighting for the next century. Due process is putting out the notice, and the contestation will last a week. You and your brother will battle the challengers independently. If one of the challengers wins against either of you, they'll fight whoever is left, and at the end of the rounds, if you and your brother defeat all combatants, you'll still face off against each another."

Dax remained calm, stone-faced, despite the heaviness weighing his chest. This situation had stretched on far too long for his people, and now they'd be subjected to another week of turbulence where they wouldn't know if either brother of the Silver Springs pack would lead. At least if Drew was distracted in fighting other folks, he wouldn't be dropping any more surprise attacks on their doorstep. What choice did Dax have?

"I accept," Dax said, his voice echoing through the hush of the bar. If the Tribe required this, he would fight until his last breath to bring the Silver Springs pack together under one leader again. He reached out, and Big and Brawny clapped a hand over his as they shook.

"Well met, Dax Williams," he said with the smirk from before curling his lips. "I'm Lucas Diaz. You've got the composure of an alpha. Let's see if you've got the endurance."

As Dax met the man's eyes, understanding dawned on him as to why the Tribe would choose this trial. This wasn't a free-for-all for any bastard setting their eye on his territory and people. Truth be told, anyone with a home wouldn't fight as fiercely as those who were at risk of losing theirs. These battles would test his stamina and strength. They would also reaffirm his commitment to his pack and his willingness to last under the hurdles that came with leadership. Dax nodded, grabbing his pint and slamming it back as his mountain lion rumbled in response to the oncoming threat. He would defend the members of Silver Springs with his life—for them, he would endure.

The rest of the Tribe finished their pints, a chorus of gulps and the clatter of empty glasses as the bottoms slammed against the hardwood table. Sierra's gaze hadn't strayed from him, a curiosity in her eyes drawing him in. He'd been fighting for his place in his family and his pack for the entirety of his life—one more week wouldn't break him. What he wasn't used to was the solid support Sierra provided, even when she didn't say a damn word. All too quickly he'd come to see why her pack would follow her to their deaths.

"We'll head out to investigate the pipe bomb issue involving your brother Drew, and tomorrow morning, we meet at the contested land for the first challengers," Navi said. Her chair squeaked against the floor as she stood. At that, the rest of the Tribe rose with a couple of glances and nods in his direction.

"Thanks, Jess. I'll see you at the matches," Sierra said as she leaned in to begin grabbing the empties. Dax jumped in to help, and a second later Finn joined them. As fast as they'd arrived, the Tribe members wasted no time in exiting, their movements as silent as the predators which marked them. The moment the door clicked shut, all their sheer power departing, tension deflated from Dax in one quick sweep. He wasn't the only one. Both Finn and Sierra lost the sharp edge to their movements.

"Now, I get why people fear those fuckers." Finn broke the silence of the room as he dragged the first batch of the glasses to the sink. "I've never met that sort of rugburn-raw intensity before. How do you know one of them?" he asked, casting a glance to Sierra.

Sierra shrugged. "Met her when I was younger, before I left Philly."

Finn nodded at Dax. "Sucks about the whole tournament you've got to go through to earn your place."

Dax's brows lifted in surprise at the sympathy from the Red Rock who'd bared teeth at him mere days ago. "Just have to tangle with a mess of shifters out for blood. No biggie, right?"

Sierra's lips turned up with a smirk. "Sorry, kitty cat. You might be outclassed. You're talking shifters in the prime of their condition—full fighting capacity."

Dax's jaw clenched on instinct. "And I'm not?" He kept his voice as bland as possible even though the lion in him roared at the slight. Before his temper slipped, he caught the twinkle in her eye and put the pieces together. She was goading him on.

"All I'm saying is you need a couple of new moves if you're going to take on other alphas in the region," she said with a casual shrug.

"If you wanted to jump me, darling, all you needed to do was ask." A broad grin spread on his face.

Finn snorted and tossed his hand in the air. "I'll let you two flirt in peace. Catch you guys bright and early—no way in hell I'm missing the fights." The wolf shifter strolled out of the place post haste, his long strides carrying him far, fast. Not like Dax blamed him for vacating the premises. He'd be lying if he said his attraction to Sierra wasn't as heavy as the scent of beer in this bar.

Sierra glanced his way, her gaze scorching. He couldn't help the way he rose to attention at the mere sight of her, at the way the two of them stood in this tavern with no interruptions. The idea of hoisting her on the bar and fucking her into oblivion dominated most of his thoughts, since the troubles looming on his horizon would multiply if he gave them the chance.

"If you're rusty on your techniques, we could spar at my place." She trailed her fingertips along the tabletop as she spoke. Dax's brows lifted because for the life of him, he couldn't tell if she meant actual sparring or the between-the-sheets action that revved his engine right now. Her gaze pinned him on the spot, freezing the smile on his lips. "Before you spout some smartass line, I mean sparring. If you're going to be fighting all week, you'd better be prepared, and I've got the lowdown on most of the beaters in this area."

"If I didn't know better, I'd think you cared," he drawled, leaning against one of the pillars. "Consider me flattered, Kanoska." Not like he was lying there. That she'd spent time and effort on a screw-up like him in the first place meant more than she could ever know.

"Don't think I'll take it easy on you just because you have a pretty face," Sierra called as she sauntered to the door, swinging her key ring around her finger with a jangle. Dax watched the sway of those hips, nearly salivating as he pushed off the pillar and hurried to follow. Despite the way she railed at him, she had to know she was driving him to her place with no ride home. If anything would test his resolve to keep the bond from turning into a noose around his neck, this would be it.

Those lithe legs for his freedom, apparently.

Chapter Eleven

Inviting Dax Williams into her house ranked up there in her history of poor decisions.

Even though the mating bond loomed over them, she could feel him buzzing with tension in the bar, and, like the other night, she couldn't help herself. He made sense to her when so many folks didn't. Besides, rage curled in her stomach at the idea of him having to jump through more hoops to keep his land after what his pack had suffered last night. She stepped up to the familiar outline of her cottage, an ivy-tangled one-bedroom deal she'd always dreamed of as a kid growing up in the city.

A shudder rolled down her spine at the memories she tried to repress. Shifters were meant for wide-open spaces, for fresh earth and looming trees. Not the narrow alleys and the cramped Section Eight housing she'd grown up in. Her wolf had been caged for far too long, and the moment she'd saved enough, she'd driven off and hadn't looked back. She'd left the shattered bottles and venomous words behind and didn't regret her decision for a second.

He pressed a palm against her shoulder, the heat of him drawing her to the present. "Everything okay?" His smooth-as-sin voice came from behind her. She fiddled with her keys to unlock the door before turning the ornate brass knob.

"I don't get many visitors," she admitted. Most of the times when she hung out with her packmates, she lingered around her place of business, Beaver Tavern, or the communal cabin they all shared. This was her sacred space, her retreat away from being an alpha. Whatever impulse pushed her to drive Dax here, already she regretted it. Yet as they stood with his hand still on her shoulder, her hormones took the wheel. The marching beat of their attraction rose by the second. She could feel his proximity, the controlled strength behind his careful touch, and her wolf lunged to mark him every time they met. Sierra might have discipline, she might have self-control, but she wasn't a goddamned saint.

His shadow fell over her. "Are we going to stand around in the door here? I thought you wanted to kick my ass, soldier," he said, aiming a light punch to her biceps. Right, a good brawl would provide the exact sort of distraction to get her head out of the gutter.

"Come on in," she responded, not bothering to look back as she plunged into her house. The lavender sachets she left tucked in cushions and drawers did their job, their delicate aroma weaving through the room. The desk she'd been trying to build lay sprawled across her hardwood floor, newspaper still laid down and the pieces scattered. Not like she'd had down time as of late. "Comment about the mess, and I'll let my claws slip when we brawl," she muttered, running a hand through her hair.

"Violent, violent woman," he purred. She didn't even need to turn back to know a wicked smile graced his lips again, the amused heat in his tone conveying everything. "If you think that'll scare me away, guess again."

Even as she hurried through her house, having someone else in her space made her skin prickle, as if she stood before him bare. Most of the pack didn't know the clear lines of delineation she'd drawn between her time as pack leader and anything personal. She loved her people with an unparalleled fierceness, but some bruises from her past had never healed, and some scabs lay one conversation away from ripping raw again.

Sierra reached the kitchen leading to her back door, even though she had to swerve around a couple of piles of mail she'd thrown on the floor, and the bag of laundry spilling into the living room. Her hand rested on the battered doorknob, ready to lead the way to the backyard, when she turned to face him. His gaze burned into her with an intensity that made her shiver; a crease formed between his furrowed brows.

"You're buzzing like you downed an entire pot of coffee," he said, his voice quiet and for once without the teasing that defined him. "Did I do something to piss you off?"

Shame flushed through her. So much for keeping a tab on her emotions. All his earnest attention might be focused her way, but she wasn't ready to go under the microscope for anyone. Sierra straightened, lifting her chin as she opened the back door.

"I don't invite people to my place," she admitted, letting the implication hang there. "Ever." Already vulnerability grew to a roar in the back of her mind, a paranoia that spread like a virus.

Dax's blue eyes darkened with understanding as he nodded in response. Sierra held her breath. The instinct to run pulsed under her skin and, if he pushed, she wouldn't be able to control the urge. Instead, he grabbed the top of the door, pushed it open wider and muscled past her, down her rickety steps and out onto grass.

"I think you're just nervous to take me on," he teased. Yet as their eyes met, she understood he dove in for her sake, covering up the vulnerability with the same care he did his own.

She took the chance to recover and flashed her teeth with a smile. "You wish. Time to stop talking, and see what you're made of."

Her steps creaked as she strode down to her backyard, which sprawled into the fringe of the woods. The proximity to the wild sated her wolf and the freedom of deep forests and the rolling fields kept her sane. The sun beat on her skin, which had darkened to a deep bronze, and a sprinkling of buttercups glowed neon in the afternoon intensity. Dax stripped off his shirt with a familiar ease, the sun illuminating his tanned skin and taut muscles. As far as distractions went, she didn't mind this one at all.

"Human or shifted form?" he asked.

Sierra snorted. "If I wolf out, you won't stand a chance. Let's run drills in human form for now." What she didn't say was if she shifted and gave the wolf even a bit of an edge, she was liable to lose her mind and jump his bones. Not like her human side did a great job reining in those impulses either.

A smile spread on his face, one that made his eyes twinkle as if another smartass remark was about to descend. She stripped her shirt off, down to her sports bra and shorts—that shut him up. The air thickened between them, a mixture of the sexual tension curling in her core and the urge to fight pounding her bones. Even in her human form, parts of her shifter self remained, the wolf so intrinsic that she padded around with a similar vigilance, a predator's caution.

Dax circled her, languid amusement in his gaze. He didn't have the bracing nature of a wolf—this mountain lion teased with a patience in his approach she couldn't hope to match. Those muscles flexed with every motion, drawing her attention to his movements. Her pulsing desire took a backseat to the predatory instinct that rode her as she waited for him to give an indication of his first move or, better yet, an opening.

He continued to circle, the slow movements sparking her nerves which bristled with anticipation. She scanned the ground around him, searching for a dip in the dirt or patch of uneven grass where he might shift footing. Knowing the mountain lion, he'd trail around her forever, trying to tire her out or bait her into going first. So, when she dove in, her first move would have to be a good one.

Not like the tactic wasn't sound. Already, her muscles begged for action, and the wolf in her readied to snap.

A bird whistled in the background, and his gaze flicked in that direction. Only for a second, but a second was all she needed. Sierra lunged.

* * * *

Sierra stretched her arms over her head, a grin spreading wide on her face. Sweat rolled down her biceps, matting her hair, and the late afternoon sun showed no sign of relenting. Dax's shoulders heaved up and down, but a smile was plastered across his face, the joy of unwinding through a good sparring session unparalleled for her kind. She hoped by fighting out the tension winding through her body she could get back in control, yet the moment their gazes locked, familiar warmth coiled in her core, a pulse between her legs that begged to be sated.

"Is this where you boot me out and tell me to run the rest of the way home?" Dax asked, sauntering past her toward the cottage. Even though she'd been in full contact with him as they'd sparred, her mind had transitioned into a different zone during the fight. Watching him stride up her stairs into her place with those delicious defined back muscles on full display punched her in the gut. Something about him in this space felt all too right and she'd be lying if that didn't scare the hell out of her.

"This is where we get some grub," she said, following him into her place. "After a workout like that, I'm jonesin' for a pulled pork sandwich." Sierra walked into her bedroom, wiping down her body with a towel. Dax's shadow spilled across her floor, drawing her gaze up. She fixed him with a look. "That wasn't an invitation to watch me change."

He smirked, pushing up from where he leaned against the doorframe to wander through her house. "Nothing I haven't seen before," he called, his voice echoing through her small cottage.

Sierra tugged on her shirt so hard at the comment she almost ripped the fabric. Her brows narrowed on instinct, the man's ability to get under her skin formidable. "You want to stop off for food? I know better places than the shithole you dragged us to."

She slipped on a maxi skirt and popped on a pair of sandals, since she didn't plan on running through any forests—at least not in this form. When she stepped out of her room, Dax stood by the mantle. He ran a finger along the surface of the porcelain animals she'd placed there, remnants of the home she'd left behind. Her hands balled into fists on instinct and a sharp sound came from her throat before she could rein it back in.

He glanced up. "You okay?" he asked, removing his hand at once. "Didn't realize they were valuable."

Sierra shook her head. "Not worth anything in that sense."

He nodded, and the tension dissolved when he slapped a smartass grin on. "So, where are you taking me on this date?" he asked, dipping his hands in his pockets as he thrust his hips forward.

Sierra clenched her jaw for a moment before responding. "We're grabbing food. That in no way constitutes a date. Invite whoever you want to join, see if I give a damn."

Dax tugged his shirt over his head. "So, you want me to bring a date?" he asked. "Let me call Ally up." Fierce heat thudded through her, the blinding sort that pulsed behind her eyes. His eyes twinkled in amusement. "Careful, you're growling."

"Let's go," she huffed, striding to the door and not waiting to see if he followed. The mating bond went to her head, messing with her control. Once they stepped outside, she locked up and Dax hopped into the car.

When they interacted as alphas, she could relate—that encouragement and camaraderie came naturally for her. However, she'd stepped on too many past landmines in relationship territory and anytime their conversations turned this way, she couldn't help trying to dodge the vulnerability prickling under her skin. Yet the fighter part of her protested, the part the abuse and past disappointment hadn't managed to snuff out of existence. The idiotic voice of hope that this time might be different.

Sierra hopped into the driver's seat, aware of the way his gaze glided over her the moment she got inside.

The impulse to fuck, to claim, pounded in her every breath, enhanced by the way they'd sparred together. Enhanced by this proximity plus the scent of mountain lion and cedar that put her brain on the fritz and drove her wolf wild. Sierra veered onto the road, throwing all the energy brewing between them into pounding on the gas pedal.

Instead of the normal right turn on the highway toward the Beaver Tavern, she took a left. Within minutes of zooming across the asphalt, the turn she knew by heart appeared. She often escaped to this bar when she'd had enough of strutting around as alpha for one night, when she needed to clear her mind in a different setting than racing through the woods. The red neon lights were on since the sunlight was waning in early evening. Sierra pulled into the lot, gravel and dust kicked up in the wake of the car.

"If you want somewhere private, we could always go to the woods," Dax purred, the sound of his voice stroking her core and igniting her temper in one sweep.

"Food. We're going for food," she repeated. "Unless you're planning on killing and cooking a rabbit or some venison out there, I'm not seeing how a jaunt through the woods is going to help."

He snorted in response, hopped out of her car and strode to the bar like he owned the place. Sierra heaved a sigh and followed.

Jarrod's Taproom was painted black from top to bottom, with dozens of windows and a couple of dim overhead lights inside separating the shadows around the joint. The owner liked it that way—even though the place was human-owned and dominated, more than a couple of shifters from the different packs came here to escape their drama. Not like bringing Dax here provided any sort of escape.

She muscled past him to enter first, throwing a hand up in acknowledgment to Rachel, the waitress by the host stand. With a wink, Rachel led them to one of the corner booths, knowing Sierra's preference for her frequent attendance. The scent of pine and mouthwatering barbecue drifted through the place, the grills and smokers in full swing.

"Thanks, Rache." Sierra gave her a nod as she took the menus from the girl and slid into the seat. The AC didn't blast here, more leaked through the air in wisps, enough to choke out the humidity trailing in while the dim lighting of the joint helped the place feel cool. Dax slipped into the opposite seat, eyeing her as if she ranked as the top choice on the menu.

"I recommend anything from the grill or the pit," she murmured, giving the menu a once-over before she went with her tried-and-true pulled pork sandwich. While the place supposedly couldn't compare to bona fide Southern cooking, she'd take the juicy, tangy meat from here any day of the week.

He scanned the menu for a minute, not looking up as he responded. "What's with the buried past, Kanoska? That seems more my avoidance drill than yours." Even though his tone remained light, the question hung in the air, the one she'd been expecting after all her twitchiness back at the cabin. Not like she disagreed with him—she preferred to lay most things out on Front Street. However, this burn from her past refused to heal, one that held no resolution.

"Let's do a care-and-share, then," she challenged. "You dive into all your daddy issues and I'll dredge up my family history from Philly."

His gaze sharpened, pinning her, as seriousness descended between them like a storm cloud. "Not fair, Kanoska. You already know my shit, but I don't have a cent of yours." He kept his voice level, feline calm an ever-present part of him, but she could feel the way he burned behind the mask.

When the king of avoidance stopped playing games, she knew she was in trouble. Keeping her past quiet had been an isolating burden, and the more she'd shared with Dax, the more they worked together, the more she realized how deep the loneliness dwelled. The comfort his presence provided, the natural way they flowed together spoke to her in volumes. For the first time, confiding her past didn't terrify her the way it should've. For the first time, she wanted to take that free fall—to let him in.

Rachel chose that moment to pop in with water and a soda, taking their orders with a whip-fast pace. Just as quickly, she flitted off to help the next customers making their way in. Sierra lifted the hot coffee to her lips to take a sip before she broke the silence.

"I didn't come out until I was a teenager, when I hopped in my car and left home. I knew more shifters lived in this region, and a couple of wolf packs roamed here. The old Red Rock alpha took me in at once. Life in the boonies took a big adjustment since I'd grown up in cramped city apartments." The memories of the home she left behind thudded in the back of her mind, the combination of sweet and bitter a brew she didn't want to swallow.

"Bad home life?" he asked.

Bile rose in her throat, but she pushed through anyway. "The bullshit part was my parents were sweet as can be. All the kindness in the world doesn't amount to shit, though, when they turned a blind eye to the scars my older brother left. Asshole wanted target practice, and I happened to be around." The words gummed up her mouth. Dax's eyes flashed, his gaze burning hot and furious for a moment. The one indication he gave was the way his claws surfaced, biting into the hardwood table.

Sierra lifted her hands, needing to re-collect her pride. She didn't want anyone's pity. "Hey, I made it through stronger and gave the guy a couple of scars of his own to remember me by. When I left, I didn't look back, but the cottage was the first home I made for myself—I give most of myself to my pack, but that and my history—that's mine."

"Brothers are a bitch, right?" Dax smiled, even though his eyes blazed. He'd sheathed his claws just in time, because Rachel approached with two plates, one laden with the juicy pulled pork slathered in their secret brown sugar sauce, and the other a roast beef sandwich dripping on the plate. Sierra's stomach rumbled at the sight.

"Here's your usual," Rachel said with a smile. "Dig in."

Sierra nodded her appreciation before plunging in. The sweet tang of the sauce spread across her tongue, melding with the spice of the pepperjack. She had to keep herself from moaning out loud. Dax tackled his sandwich with the same desperation. Their type needed to fuel up more than most, and after the way they'd burned calories earlier, they'd both earned the meals. Within the span of minutes, the contents of their plates lay destroyed before them, the sandwiches a distant memory.

"So, are you ready for tomorrow?" Sierra asked, wiping the remains of the sauce from her mouth.

Dax leaned back in his seat with his hands behind his head, putting those defined triceps on full display. "As ready as I'm going to be. If this is the path I have to take to get my land and my pack back, so be it." His determination resonated with her, with the shared fierce protectiveness for their packs.

Sierra pulled out her wallet and dropped cash on the table. "I've got this."

Dax swatted her cash out of the way, then grabbed his own wallet. "Bullshit, you do. You carted my ass around all day and gave my pack support when we needed help the most. This is one drop in the bucket of what I owe you." He reached out, his fingertips brushing against her wrist as his gaze homed in on her. "Please, let me do this much." Even though she still felt stubborn about it, the hoarse scrape in his voice sold her.

"Fine," she said, the word coming a little more spitefully than intended. She took a deep breath and let go of her resistance. "Thank you," came out more softly.

The flirtation was one thing between them, an effortless dance she could get swept away in with ease. This back-and-forth sank its claws inside her and tugged, slicing deeper than she preferred. Even though Sierra tried to keep her distance, tried to ignore the pulse of the mating bond between them, Dax Williams had made his mark on her without fail. He was a charming smile and hot-as-hell promise at first, but the more experiences they shared and the more she revealed the hidden parts of herself, the deeper the gravity of their interactions settled in her marrow, striking a deep part of her she'd long buried.

"Let's get rolling," she rushed out, trying to ignore the thudding of her heartbeat that arrived with her realization. "You've got to be well rested for your fight." He narrowed his brows in confusion at the rush of her words, but she didn't wait around to indulge, making her way through the taproom at top speed. Dax plunked the cash on the table and followed suit, slinking behind her. The second she stepped outside, the humid summer air painted every square inch of her skin.

He grabbed her shoulder, the touch drawing her to an immediate halt. She whipped around to face him.

"You go from self-assured one second to aggressive the next." Dax stood behind her, eyes gleaming. "Look, I know the mating bond is difficult to ignore, but no one's forcing you into anything."

She stood in front of him, inches away, as the air charged between them. His blue eyes glowed in intensity, and her wolf surged, desperate to claim him.

Fuck it.

Sierra lunged in, her lips crushing against his. A growl ripped from his throat at the collision, one that hummed against her mouth. The ache inside her grew painful in its intensity, a swell more powerful than any she'd experienced before. His lips scraped against hers, his mouth hot and demanding as his big palms settled around her waist. Her grip tightened in his hair, tugging the short strands as she crashed against him again and again, demanding more.

Need surged through so strongly she could barely think, so strongly it short-circuited her functions, and all at once, she prepared to drown under the wave.

A loud pop echoed through the air, sending both of them leaping away from each other. Sierra glanced around for the source of the sound to spot a car backfiring. After the pipe bombs the night before, she still reacted on instinct.

Sierra sucked in a deep, shaky breath, not only startled but overcome by the sheer power of the emotions sweeping through her. As she glanced back and met Dax's gaze, understanding reflected there as if the same realization hit him too. When they made the step, the moment they went all the way, she couldn't turn back. They'd be mated for life. Even though the idea no longer made her bolt, it that wasn't the sort of decision to be made because her hormones accelerated into overdrive.

Dax ran a hand through his hair, his gaze skating the ground as sheepishness claimed them both.

Sierra broke through, regaining her control. "If you manage to win this thing, that's just a taste of what's coming your way," she said with a wink, projecting more assurance than she felt.

Dax cracked a smile, the light returning to his gaze. "Well, then, you better be prepared for the full onslaught once I take down these bastards challenging me." The spark of a fight flickered in his expression, one that burned through her.

She bared her teeth in defiance, even though what surfaced between them had her teetering on the edge of a canyon.

"Bring it."

Chapter Twelve

Dax had woken up at the asscrack of dawn, and while he'd only slugged one cup of coffee down, his nerves jittered as if he'd drunk the whole pot. He rolled to the cabin where Ally and the others had taken refuge in Red Rock territory, the one where he'd met Sierra for that initial meeting. Even though the attack had happened a mere day and a half ago, an age had passed in his mind. Sweat pricked on his brow as he exited the car, stepping into the swampy humidity that had already descended today.

His nerves kicked into high gear when he approached the front door, but his mind kept drifting to Sierra. As of late, she'd pounded through his head to the point of obsession. Each piece of her puzzle he uncovered had him craving more of the resilient woman with a shattered past who'd never let it conquer her. Alone in his bed last night, he'd tossed and turned, the need consuming him to the point that even roping off a couple of times hadn't taken the edge off.

Mating bond or no, the woman was the first he'd encountered who sustained his interest, who he could imagine something lasting with. Normally self-loathing would set in when they got too close, his father's reminder on replay that he'd never be good enough. Except Sierra managed to push right through with an unparalleled determination. She grounded him and strengthened him in a way no other before had.

Sucking in a breath, he entered the cabin.

"Hey, boss," Kyle called, leaning against the wall. "Heard you're going to be taking on challengers from all over."

"Testing my prowess against my brother isn't enough," Dax said, cracking a smile. "They want to make sure the Silver Springs alpha is best in the region." He didn't bother mentioning what would happen if either he or his brother failed, even though the weight of that possibility had kept him up at night. One misstep in these matches and the entire Silver Springs pack would get torn from their homes. These people he'd known his entire life could be separated.

Voices murmured throughout the place, but only six of his pack lingered in the cabin at the moment. Lana stayed with Rick, Marcy and the kids in a rental cabin while Rick healed and Lana had space to grieve for Greg. He'd already had the talk with her. They were waiting to hold the funeral until after the fights, once the future of their pack was decided. The pit in his stomach stole his attention for a moment, but he had to put on a strong front. Dax nodded at the crew, making his way to the bedroom, where Ally lay bed-bound.

"That you, Williams?" she shouted. He grinned, walking through the open door.

"Ally-cat, how're you healing up?" Dax leaned against the doorframe of the dimly lit room. Even with the sheets covering her, the wounded leg was out, wrapped and elevated.

The blonde leaned forward, trying to disguise her wince with the movement. Her expressive face had grown pale from pain while she healed. The injury she'd sustained from the explosion hadn't been minor, and that colloidal silver had made healing a bitch, as he'd suspected.

"Top shape. Is it time to rip Drew a new one yet?" Her voice was hoarse with venom. Even though she'd chosen Dax's side, the complicated history she had with his brother wasn't a secret. They'd been on and off again for a long time until Ally had enough of being treated like trash. That he'd been behind the bomb to leave her with physical scars was a cruel coincidence.

"Unfortunately, I've got to combat every asshole in the area who wants to claim leadership first. The Tribe came rolling in and throwing down proclamations." Dax crossed his arms over his chest.

Ally's mouth quirked in a smile, the look giving her more of her former edge. "Lucky you. You'll mop the floor with them."

Pride burned in his chest at the faith his pack had in him, enough that they'd separate from the rest of their kin to follow. If he had any reason to fight, these people, his real family, were enough.

His phone buzzed in his pocket, and he tugged it out to glance at the screen. Unknown number. He lifted it, hitting the button to answer.

"Dax Williams, your first challenger has stepped to the plate," Navi's voice barked over the speaker. Ally crooked a brow, able to hear from across the room.

"Any word on my brother?" Dax asked. The line fell silent for a moment.

"Look." Navi grew quieter. "The pipe bombs trace back to the reason we were in the region. While a couple of the injured placed Drew's pack on the scene, the organization we're hunting tends to draw randoms into the fold. No one could ID Drew, so he's still allowed to participate. We can't go on hearsay from a biased party."

Dax's chin jutted forward as he let out a breath of disappointment. "Understood." If the Tribe wouldn't lock away his brother for those crimes, then Dax would make sure Drew paid on the battlefield. "Who am I fighting today?"

"Dorlan Tully of the Underwood bear pack. The fight begins at noon at the Silver Springs testing ground. If you're late, you forfeit the match." At that, a click sounded as she hung up.

"Wish me luck," he said, pushing off the doorframe. "We'll be drinking tonight to celebrate my victory." Dax winked and gave a salute to acknowledge the rest of his pack as he walked through the cabin.

"We wouldn't miss it," Kyle shouted from the other room. "We want to see the bear pound your ass."

Dax shook his head, unable to hide the grin on his face as he lifted his middle finger in the air. "Laugh it up, assholes. See you at the match." He hopped out the door, his heart pounding in anticipation of the oncoming fight. The lion in him begged to launch into battle for his people, his territorial instinct strong, but the human side of him churned with unease.

One mistake, one loss, and his pack would be shattered for good—or worse, in the hands of his asshole brother.

* * * *

For the first time since the shakeup, Dax drove into the heart of his old territory without fear of retribution from his brother and the traitors. With the matches occurring, they'd be on their best behavior. Meanwhile, the Tribe sniffed around whatever secret business they'd gotten involved in. He braced his forearm against the open window of his car, the breezes rushing in to tangle his hair and paste his sweat to his skin. The urge to fight pounded a marching beat in his chest, one that made him feel knife-edge alive.

With all the worries over Drew's next move and the mating bond, focusing on winning one match dosed him with relief. The familiar trees of his forest flickered by, those knotty limbs half-leaning into the road and swaying as his truck raced along. The sun winked off the windshield as he adjusted his sunglasses. Despite the tension he and Sierra had left dangling between them, he couldn't help but wonder if she'd show to support him today.

The dirt road appeared before Dax was ready, and he made an abrupt right, his truck rumbling over the uneven path. He'd been to these training grounds a thousand times before, but the last time remained raw and battered—when he'd fought his brother for alpha and the elders he'd grown up respecting had driven him from his home.

He bounced in the seat as his truck ripped down the road, tires crunching branches or kicking around loose stone. Birds chirped while foxes and deer rustled through the surrounding brush. Their sounds melded with the brisk scent of pine and rich loam of fertile earth that tickled his nose. If Dorlan Tully wanted to try to take a bite out of him, bring it. This was his territory—his home—and he refused to give up his lands.

The old lake he'd swum in as a kid glittered ahead, and Dax slowed. A couple of cars parked in the gravel spots that had been carved out long before his time. The wind carried a foreign scent, the damp musk of the bear shifter making Dax's fangs protrude on instinct. A low, guttural growl ripped from his throat. If he glanced to the mirror, his eyes would be glowing as his beast emerged.

The old tree stumps and folding chairs they used during meetings had been pulled out to the sidelines while the beaten earth of the fighting circle remained pristine and clear. Already the five Tribe members he'd met the other day took their seats, right at the edge of the circle. A man he'd seen twice before paced in front of them, bulging arms crossed. The slope of Dorlan's ebony eyes and the thick even darker hair falling down his back in waves hinted at Cherokee heritage. The man brimmed with more aggression than Dax remembered.

He pulled his truck to a quick halt and sucked in a deep breath. Calm and cool—patience would win him this fight, not rushing in half-assed and raging. And no mistake about it, he had to win.

Sun spilled through the trees, causing the lake to glow. The sight was a reminder of easier days with him and Drew when the only fights between them revolved around who could stay underwater longer. Dax rolled his shoulders back, pushing himself to stay loose and relaxed as he strode toward the Tribe.

He didn't need to look to his left when tires crunched gravel as someone else pulled in. The moment she arrived, his body stood at attention like a tuning fork. Even as Sierra slammed the door to her car and jogged up behind him, her presence caused a prickle along his skin, an awareness he couldn't deny due to the bond between them.

"Is this the guy I'm supposed to be fighting?" Dax called out, his hands in his pockets as he strolled up to the Tribe. "When you said bear alpha, I was impressed—expecting some big, brawny thing—but instead, this beanpole shows up." He flashed his teeth with his smile, knowing in this case he poked the bear.

Dorlan growled, a deep guttural bellow threatening to rip through the place.

Dax winked at him. "Save it for the match, hot stuff." If looks could kill, he'd be dead at this point. Beyond all else, he excelled at pissing people off. What most didn't realize was that in keeping his temper, he had the advantage. Besides, serious types were all too fun to torture. He'd delighted in pressing Sierra's buttons from the moment they'd met.

"I've never seen Dorlan that irritated. You truly have a gift for annoyance," Sierra murmured as she stepped beside him. Dax delivered a half bow with a flourish of his arm. She reached out to squeeze his shoulder. "Better hone all those skills into kicking his ass. You still owe me a favor that's going to be tough to uphold if you're not alpha of the Silver Springs pack." The words were casual, as was the touch, but the scorching way she looked at him was anything but.

"Your wish is my command," he said with a salute as Navi stepped away from the rest of the Tribe. The short woman cut the fiercest presence out of the Tribe members, like bringing a flamethrower to a shooting range.

"Enough with the pleasantries," Navi cut them off. "You're not here to flirt—you're here to fight,

Williams." The sun caused her skin to glow, enhancing the contrast between the thick black lines of the tattoos marking her entire body.

He shrugged, trying not to let nerves overtake him. "Can't help if I'm talented at both." Navi crooked a brow at him, even though she fought with a twitch at her mouth threatening to turn into a smile.

"Come on, lion-boy," Dorlan muttered, making his way to the center of the thirty-foot circle. "Let's see if you can back up all your big talk."

Despite the worry marching a consistent beat in the back of his brain, Dax sucked in the sweet breath of the moisture-laden summer air and flexed his arms, relishing the way the sun's heat caressed his skin. The animalistic side of him welcomed this, the urge to mark his territory growing stronger with every step.

Dorlan faced him on the other side of the ring, his silence palpable.

Dax never liked ceremony, and too much seriousness grated on his nerves, but he'd have to be beyond stupid to mouth off too much in front of the Tribe. Even though he stood a chance against the big ole alpha from Underwood, every member of the Tribe, from pint-size Navi to big-beater Lucas, could thrash his ass into next Sunday. So he rolled his shoulders instead and faced his opponent, sizing up the asshole from Underwood who figured he could take a bite out of him.

"Shifted or human form?" Dax asked, glancing to the Tribe members who sat in their lawn chairs as if they were holding fucking court. Though in their case, they pretty much were. The size and strength of your beast reflected the individual, but with the way Dorlan's eyes burned, this serious bastard planned on throwing all his weight into this match. Seeing him in action would tip off if he had reflexes to back up the brawn.

"Territory is the animal's right," Lucas said, his voice booming across the terrain. "So, this challenge will be in your shifted forms." He regarded both of them with his palms out and hands spread wide. At the announcement, Dax kicked off his loose pants and tossed his shirt out of the way while Dorlan followed suit.

"Dorlan Tully of the Underwood pack and Dax Williams of the Silver Springs pack, you are to face one another in combat over the terrain of the Silver Spring shifters. The first one who doesn't rise loses. The winner will advance to face the next contestant." Lucas's gaze sharpened as he regarded them.

Dax's muscles tensed, waiting for the impending signal.

"Ready?" his voice boomed, the air thickening. Cars pulled up in the interim. Closing doors and crunching gravel echoed over to where Dax stood. More folks approached the clearing by the minute, but the noise and the people had all become peripheral for Dax. Right here, right now, he focused on Dorlan while waiting for Lucas Diaz to say the word. Sweat trickled down his forehead and he flexed his fingers.

"Fight," Lucas shouted in a roar, his voice quaking the surrounding air.

At the sound of Lucas's voice, Dax shifted.

His mountain lion surged to the surface, the transition happening as fast as falling water. His fangs emerged, claws pricked out and the fur coated his skin as his bones began to meld in different directions. Within the span of a second, he no longer stood on two feet, but rather crouched on all four.

Ahead of him, Dorlan shifted into a hulking black bear, the fur ink-stain dark, and those eyes shrewd. The air around them turned as tense as a thundercloud as they began to circle the clearing. Shifters from the Red Rocks, Silver Springs and Dorlan's pack surrounded them on all sides, watching the match—most had a stake in the outcome. As the mountain lion, he could feel his people on the peripheral, presences who'd become his family over the years. And of course, he felt her there in attendance, her appearance bolstering his confidence.

Dorlan's back paw kicked off. The motion snapped Dax's focus to the forefront, but his muscles bristled at attention. The bear barreled for him, lumbering with the force of a falling tree trunk. Dax swerved back and forth in a radius of a couple of feet, not giving the bear a direct target to focus on. Even though Dorlan rushed for him like a juggernaut, Dax didn't duck out of the way. Not yet.

He kept weaving, back and forth, back and forth as Dorlan thundered toward him, closer and closer. Dax's heart hammered in his chest as his paws pounded a rhythm on the beaten earth.

Dorlan launched forward, feet away from him.

At the last second, Dax leaped to the right—out of the way. Dorlan skidded to a halt in the spot Dax had just been, kicking up dirt and pebbles in the process. Speed was of the essence. Seizing the seconds granted, he whipped around and sank his claws into Dorlan's flank. The black bear growled, a thunder that quaked the earth around them, but before he could turn around the entire way, Dax disappeared from the spot, slinking away.

As he'd thought. *Slow reflexes.*

Dax sprinted to the opposite side of the clearing, resuming his predatory pace while he waited for the next charge.

Out of the corner of his eye, he caught sudden motion.

As quick as a snap, Dorlan charged.

The massive bear hurtled for him at the shorter distance, giving him less reaction time. Dax snapped to attention, whipping around to his side and veering to the right. Closer, closer. The stench of wet bear weighed heavy in the air, and the beast's hot breath came out in a blast. Dax swerved out of the way, right as one of those massive paws sailed straight for him.

He didn't move fast enough.

The edge of the paw slammed into him, the weight tossing him back even as several of those claws sank in past his fur, drawing blood. Dax growled as he darted away, a trail of red droplets dripping along the beaten earth. He'd gotten too cocky. He needed skill and speed, but all Dorlan required was a lucky swipe to conk him upside the head.

Before Dorlan whipped around, Dax switched to the offensive.

He lunged forward, teeth bared as he dove straight for the exposed neck.

His teeth sank in, past the skin, the puncture echoing through the air with a crunch. Dorlan thrashed, sending both of them careening sideways. Dax released his hold, flowing with the motion rather than resisting as he smacked against the earth before tumbling away. He'd long ago learned to use his opponents' attacks against them, and following rather than defending attacks gave him a risky edge. Blood flowed freely from the exposed patch of flesh, matting the black fur around Dorlan's neck.

Rage flashed in the Underwood alpha's eyes, the sort promising retribution.

Dax rose to his paws as he started to circle again. *Good. Get angry. Get stupid.* He was just beginning to have fun.

Chapter Thirteen

Sweat trickled down Sierra's back, having nothing to do with the blistering day. Her fists clenched as Dorlan and Dax went toe-to-toe inside the arena. She wasn't the only one watching in loaded silence. Members of the Silver Springs pack had shown up, including a couple of the idiots who'd chased Dax out. She recognized the older one Dax called Uncle Aiden, though the woman he'd been with earlier, Rylie, hadn't shown her face.

The Tribe watched from their seats with the stony faces of judgment Sierra had expected. She'd seen Jess in action before, her jaguar as lethal as her human form with a spirit-given magic for manipulating the air around her. Somehow having a squad of them here made the situation graver. They would stand witness to justice even if the fight grew brutal. Even if it became life-threatening. Sierra's throat dried as she tried to swallow the fear choking her veins.

Dorlan pawed at the ground, the big black bear radiating uncontrolled fury. Some might find the massive shifter formidable, but Sierra was much more impressed by the cool tension emanating from Dax's mountain lion. Even his attack, the quick swipes to irritate and wear his opponent down, reflected the man she'd come to know. Go figure, that happened to be his same style of flirtation as well—annoy her half to death until, before she could stop herself, she confessed her deep darks and bonded with him to a degree she never had before. A half smile rose to her lips, one she shook off.

Dax coiled around the bear, his circles growing tighter and tighter. Every time Dorlan charged, Dax would bide his time, veering away at the last minute. However, he left less space each time, closer and closer to a lethal attack.

While Jess and Lucas watched from their lawn chairs with a hungry interest, Navi had begun picking her nails with her knife and Akio feigned disinterest, even though his gaze kept slipping to the scene. Jareth's eyes appeared closed in slumber, but Sierra had the feeling if anyone tried to get the jump on him, the trespasser would be sorely outmatched. Whatever reason the Tribe had to be in the area, this was clerical work along the way to something much bigger.

Dorlan roared, blood leaking from his side and rage blooming in his eyes. Sierra predicted Dax's attempt, because she would've pulled the same maneuver. Except compared to his obnoxious feline patience, even she came off like a hothead. The bear charged again, kicking up dust in the process. Grit roiled all around, carried by the breeze to spray out against the audience.

Coughs peppered the place, and Sierra lifted her arm over her mouth for cover.

Through the clouds of dust, Dorlan charged Dax, driven by reckless rage. While the bear alpha had immense weight on his side, he was slower, clumsier, and Dax took ruthless advantage. The cat wove back and forth until the bear veered too close to stop, then Dax rerouted. With liquid smoothness, he swerved to the left.

Right as Dorlan swiped in the same direction.

Sierra's hands balled into fists. If Dorlan surged too fast for Dax to escape, he'd get mauled.

Dax ducked.

Instead of retreating, instead of circling out of the way again, the mountain lion lunged in. He rammed his skull straight into Dorlan's neck.

The sound of impact echoed throughout the clearing, and relief swept Sierra in one quick flush. Dorlan swayed on his feet, but Dax didn't give him any quarter. The mountain lion whipped around to slam his full weight into the bear's side, sending him toppling. Once he seized the advantage, Dax pinned him down.

He rested one pad over his windpipe, the claws close to biting past skin. Dax kept his gaze trained on Dorlan, who thrashed, attempting to breathe. The gasps and wheezes sounded painful and Sierra couldn't help but wince. She'd been in chokeholds before. Dax had the advantage.

Their eyes met and the bear nodded.

Dax lessened the pressure against his throat so he could breathe, but didn't get off him, nor did Dorlan struggle. Dax cast his gaze over to the Tribe.

Lucas got up from his neon-green lawn chair with a creak and walked to the center of the clearing. Lifting his hands, he began the count.

Dax didn't shift in the slightest, his claws out in case Dorlan decided at the last second to give it another go. With the way Dax positioned himself, he could slice the bear's throat open then and there.

"Aaaaaaand one," Lucas boomed, sweeping his hands out. "I hereby declare Dax Williams of the Silver Springs pack the winner."

The loyal Silver Springs watching in the crowds erupted in powerful roars that quaked the air. Swept up in the relief and euphoria of Dax's victory, Sierra lifted her head to the sky and howled, the cry of her wolf piercing the clearing. Her pack followed suit until the howls and the roars meshed together in one furious melody.

Both Dax and Dorlan shifted to their human forms, stark naked in the clearing. Dax flashed a quick smile to the crowds, the slick sort she expected from him. Leaning down, he offered a hand to help Dorlan up.

"Tough luck, man," he said as the bear alpha accepted the assist.

"You could have killed me, but you didn't," Dorlan responded, putting his hand out to shake. "The Underwood pack will remember that kindness when you're alpha of the Silver Springs pack."

Dax grunted in response, slapping his palm against the bear alpha's and shaking. Neither man said anything more, but instead they strode toward the crowds, leaking blood from the myriad cuts and wounds they'd garnered during their fight. The members of the Underwood clan in the crowd rushed to their alpha, towels in hand.

Even though she didn't have the same reasons as Dax's pack to approach, Sierra couldn't help herself. Kyle and the others raced ahead of her, but the accelerated thump-thump in her chest wouldn't calm until she knew none of the wounds were life-threatening. Injuries might also set him back in a future fight. The worry that had run rampant through her during the fight had traveled deeper than normal, another indicator of how he'd infected her.

Even with all the folks surrounding him, Dax met her eyes. The small smile he flashed her pierced straight through her heart, more raw and real than any of the flirty grins he offered the crowds and his pack. Her heart thundered to the forefront of her focus, making her all too aware of the flush traveling up her skin at the memory of yesterday and the barriers they'd begun to break down.

"Exciting fight, right, boss?" Finn clapped a hand on her back, drawing her focus away from Dax for a moment. "Why don't we prep to celebrate his victory back at the tavern?"

Sierra studied Finn for a moment. With the insistent way he glanced at his car, he had more than prepping the tavern on his mind. Chances were he wanted answers, and as her second-in-command, she owed him some real talk.

"Let's go," she said with a nod. Tossing a hand up, she called to the crowd, "Red Rock, Underwood, Silver Springs pack and any Tribe members who like, we'll be celebrating with drinks back at the Beaver Tavern tonight." Even though she longed to turn around, push through the crowd and run her hands over every inch of Dax, for the time being she had enough self-control. Besides, the second she slid her fingers across those defined abs of his, the urge to jump his bones would overrule reason.

Finn had driven her and Jer here, so she hopped into the passenger side of his Challenger, glancing around.

"He's going to catch up later," Finn said, tilting his head out to where Jer was chatting up more than a couple of the Silver Springs ladies. He'd already whipped out the bedroom smile and chances were Streaky had some more one-nighters in his future. Sierra smirked, leaning back in her seat. Finn started the car and peeled out, kicking up dust and leaves as he exited the clearing.

Silence descended between them, and not the familiarity she'd grown used to. This loaded kind dropped down like a lead weight.

"Finn, you've known me too long to play coy. What the hell's got you all tangled up?" Sierra glanced to where he hunched forward, grip tight on the steering wheel, so unlike the easy way he usually drove this thing. She'd been in the car with him enough to know when something was eating him up inside.

"This is one of those blurred lines," he said. "There's shit that's my business as beta, and shit that's your personal life. I prefer not to cross the two, but I'm sensing there's something more going on between you and a certain alpha than you're telling me about." Finn glanced over quick before he exited the winding back roads and merged onto the highway. "While he doesn't seem like a bad sort, this is involving other packs now, which makes it my problem too. I need to know what's going on with you."

Sierra sucked in a harsh breath. Not like she'd been inconspicuous with all the time she'd been spending with Dax lately. Still, she hadn't solidified her own decision on that, let alone figured out where he stood with their whole situation. Both of them danced along the ledge, neither willing to take the plunge.

"Don't see me digging into your will-they-won't-they with Raven, even though you're both pack, do you?" she retorted. "Could turn the same logic around and ask you to clarify your intentions with our favorite bartender."

"You could because she's pack. He isn't." Finn gripped the wheel tighter. "Don't make this harder than it already is, boss."

The low thrum of Finn's favorite obnoxious electronica filtered through the speakers. She'd gone to a session at his kickboxing studio and left it at one. If she'd wanted to go to a club, she would've stayed in Philly. He pressed his lips tightly, the slight flush of irritation reaching all the way through his buzz cut and accentuating the scar that sliced through his right brow. The scar she'd given him back when they'd fought for alpha.

"Fuck me," Sierra complained, running her fingers through her hair.

Finn snorted. "We've tried that tango before—didn't work then, don't think it would now."

She couldn't help the smile that rose to her face. Even though she might keep her damaged past from these guys, the Red Rock pack was her present, her future and her home. "The mating bond cropped up. Dax and I are meant to be mates." She wanted to gulp those words back, but they lay in the air, brazen between them. Her own feelings on the situation might be endlessly complex, but the immediate issue and Finn's concern wasn't.

Finn let out a low whistle. "You're mated to one of the kitty cats? I would've sworn you'd find some submissive little thing or a mean motherfucker of a wolf. Never in a million years could I see you with a slick-talking feline like him."

"I need a smoke." Sierra flipped open the glove compartment and grabbed the emergency pack he kept there. She snagged one of the cigarettes as he passed over the lighter from his pocket. This old habit cropped up whenever she got too stressed, even though she'd made good headway on quitting most of the time. After lighting the cig, she took a deep drag before letting a stream of smoke out the window. Quick as a snap, the lull of nicotine flooded through her veins.

"So, what are you planning on doing?" he asked, zooming along the highway at top speed. Strong breezes coiled through the car, threatening to tug her cigarette away.

"Damned if I know. We haven't solidified the bond yet—both parties have to be in agreement. I mean shit, what if we did? We're alphas of separate packs and, worse, he's a mountain lion, so merging the packs is out of the question. We'd have to form an alliance or something." She tapped the spare ash out the window before taking another drag. "Just met the guy and I've got one too many scars to ride off into the sunset with a stranger."

"The guy's a royal pain in the ass," Finn said, one-handedly nabbing a cig from the pack and slipping it in his mouth. Sierra murmured her agreement. "However, I've seen you pour every ounce of yourself into leading this pack for a long time now. If you've met someone who can share the burden, hell, the shot at a mate most of us will never get? Don't let fear rob you of the chance."

"Easy for you to say," she muttered. "When are you going to cement things with Raven?"

He blew a stream of smoke out of the window as he shrugged. "Maybe never. We have fun, but she's not my mate or anything."

Sierra nodded, keeping her opinions to herself. Might be a bit of fun for Finn, but with the lovesick way Raven watched him, the girl was in too deep.

Finn's dark eyes were serious for once when he glanced at her. "Whatever you choose, just know I'm backing you."

Warmth flooded her chest like liquid sunshine at the pride and love she had for her pack, for her beta. Even though she'd spent her entire childhood feeling like no one batted in her corner, the Red Rock pack had rallied behind her, creating an unshakeable foundation that made even the toughest battles worth fighting. With Finn and the others by her side, she'd untangle this mess.

The familiar shape of the Beaver Tavern rose in the distance, and Finn slowed as he pulled off the highway and into the unpaved parking lot.

He tossed his car into park and offered a hand in her direction. "Ready to get this place ready for celebrating?"

Sierra clapped her hand over his. "Last one to the bar gets stuck doing dishes."

* * * *

Sierra and Finn spent a couple of hours bringing in the extra shipments of Yuengling they had delivered and tossing up a few blue-and-red streamers for decoration. At last, the bar opened. Seamus ran the taps and Jer was pulling into the parking lot with two Silver Springs girls who had driven him over. *Not as though that shocks anyone. New week means the pack lawyer trolls for a new piece of arm candy.* Sierra stood outside the bar, watching the dusky amber rays of late afternoon roll in.

She lifted the beer bottle to her lips and took a sip of the icy lager, savoring the sweetness before she swallowed. Her heartbeat picked up a couple of notches and she refused to lie to herself—Dax was the reason. They'd ditched fast after his fight, before she'd gotten to swap a sentence with him, and she wanted to congratulate him by her lonesome. The talk with Finn had her juiced, giving her the courage toward that final step.

She spotted his truck along the highway, the black truck she'd driven with him in the day they'd gotten in the scuffle with his family.

He veered into the drive, sending up a spray of gravel as he screeched into a spot.

The bar door rattled, drawing her attention away from Dax's appearance as Finn stepped out, a dishtowel slung over his right shoulder. He pulled out a cigarette and offered the pack. Sierra nabbed one, still on her kick from earlier. They both lit up, clouds of smoke trickling out past the porch into the soaked, humid air.

Dax hopped out of his truck and shut the door behind him, the sound echoing throughout the clearing. A couple more cars crunched into the parking lot, more of the Silver Springs pack from earlier. When Dax's blue eyes descended on her, a low growl sprang from his throat, one that echoed through the air.

"Oh, fuck," Finn swore, backing away from her. Sierra tapped the ash on her cigarette before taking another draw as she glanced back and forth between Finn and Dax. "If he's in the middle of mating, he's going to be a territorial, hormonal Molotov. I'm getting the hell out of the way." Finn flicked the cigarette onto the gravel before he spun around and marched inside.

Sierra let out a low whistle. She could attest to that. If Dax had arrived with the blonde from the other day or another female packmate in his car, she couldn't have staved the impulse to bash the woman's skull in. *Not like Finn knew what pot he stirred when he called me off for a private chat.*

Dax's storm cloud marched her way, his gaze fiery and his mouth drawn tight. With the way his shoulders tensed and his hands balled into fists, first asshole to get in his face would get the ole one-two.

Sierra stepped in front of the door, crossing her arms in front of her. Looked like she'd be that asshole.

Chapter Fourteen

As if the way she'd disappeared with Finn hadn't made his stomach drop like a rollercoaster, the second he rolled up here, he saw the bastard standing there sharing a cigarette with her. Dax couldn't help but see red. His fingers itched for one good swing, but before he could launch himself at the Red Rock beta, the alpha stepped in the way. Sierra jutted her right hip out like she always did when her stubbornness took the wheel, and based on the way her brows drew together, she'd turned into immovable granite.

He snarled before he could help himself. Everything about this was stupid and insecure. Jealousy hadn't been his MO for a long time, not since his young, testosterone-fueled years. The thump-thump-thump between his ears created a war charge he found impossible to ignore. His mountain lion paced in his chest, demanding to mark his territory.

"Dax, calm the hell down," Sierra snapped, her voice drawing him to front and center. "Finn needed to know what was going on between us, because he's my beta."

"And what did you have to say on the subject?" he asked, his voice lower than normal. Despite the way he fought to rein in his temper, he couldn't quite swing unaffected and glib with his normal ease.

Sierra uncrossed her arms and stepped closer, reaching out to put a hand on his shoulder. At her touch, the pacing calmed and the thunder in his vision quieted. "I told him we're potential mates. However, if you're going to get your panties in a twist every time I talk to a male, we're going to have a problem."

His hormones still raged from the fight and from the potential one that had been averted. She stood before him with a serious look in her eyes, oblivious to how fuckable the slope of her ass was, how goddamn sexy the firm lines of her lips were. He reached out, spearing his fingers through her hair and yanking the strands back to seize control. Fuck this dance. If he didn't get his hands on her, he would go insane.

Dax descended, claiming her lips in one sweep. He drank in her honeyed taste, spice and smoke on her lips from her lager and cigarette. She let out a low moan, her tongue slipping out to slide into his mouth. He devoured her without hesitation, his one hand fisting her hair while he trailed the other down the tantalizing slope of her waist. Not like Sierra was some meek, melting thing. Her nails sank into his pec, the other hand curled around his nape as she kissed just as hard, crashing against him with the fury of the tide.

She pulled back to gasp for breath. "Dax, we shouldn't—no way in hell are we going the full way without a goddamn conversation."

"I've had it to here with talk," he growled, unwilling to drop this sort of passion yet again. He leaned in, and his teeth brushed against her ear before he nipped down. "If we're not going to fuck, then I'm at least going to taste you."

Her eyes widened and began to glitter with mischief, the sort that made her smoky looks smolder. "I can get behind that," she said, glancing over to the parking lot. "Though I think we're blocking the entryway."

At least a handful of members from both of their packs milled around the parking lot by the cars, maintaining their distance. Dax smirked, entertained by the glances sneaked their way. His lion brimmed with pride at the public way he'd staked his claim, even if the human side of him would rather keep their time private. He controlled his impulses, though his lion wanted him to mount her in this doorframe, onlookers be damned.

"Let's take this somewhere else," he said. Sierra took charge, tugging him forward with force that surprised him.

"You might as well enjoy the effort we put in setting up for at least a second," Sierra muttered as they entered the Beaver Tavern. A couple of folks loitered around the pool table, and at least three Red Rocks sat at the bar with Seamus behind the taps. Finn stood beside him, freezing when he caught sight of Dax.

Dax widened his smile, baring his teeth. The urgency to tear the man's head off was drowned by the need he had right now to drag Sierra in the back and taste every inch of her. They'd done up the tables with some confetti and streamers hung from the ceiling in lines of neon blue and engine red.

"You did this for me?" he asked, winding his arm around Sierra's shoulders. "I'll have to think of some way to repay you." His voice grew husky with intent, one mirrored in her eyes as they darkened in desire.

"Finn," Sierra called, drawing her beta's attention, "I'm nabbing the back office for a hot second."

Finn's gaze traveled from Dax to Sierra and the arm he had around her before realization dawned on the beta's face followed by a slow smile. "Enjoy yourselves."

Sierra maneuvered past the bar to the back room where a mess of steam drifted out of the dishwashers and the kitchen counters sprawled out to line the rest of the room. A younger guy worked at the sinks. Her grip didn't falter around Dax's once, and together they made their way to the adjoining office. When they entered, Sierra locked the door behind them and flipped down the wooden blinds with a *snick* that echoed through the room.

"Finally," he breathed, beginning to circle her with his predatory instinct in high gear. She leaned against the massive oak desk that took up most of the room, piled high with papers. Tension descended between them with the heaviness of an oncoming storm. Sierra's dusky gaze was glued to him as he paced in front of her, ready to pounce. The amber light streaming through the slats competed with the single lamp in the corner of the room, the rest of the place devoured by shadows.

"You going to keep dancing in front of me?" she asked, her brow lifted and the corner of her mouth quirked up. Her scent, cinnamon and smokes, enflamed him, drawing him in like an elixir. The way her hips jutted forward made him salivate, her jean shorts revealing an ample amount of bronzed skin. Dax stopped his back-and-forth, stilling as their eyes locked.

He prowled toward her and slammed his hands against the desk on either side of her. A growl came from deep in Sierra's throat, one that vibrated through the air around them. This was one woman who wouldn't go gently into the night, who would fight as furiously as he did. Her dark eyes sparked with rebellion as she stared at him, their faces and their bodies braced mere inches apart. This close, her hot breath puffed against his cheek, those full lips beckoning him yet again.

Before he could lunge forward and claim her, she surged up to crash against his lips.

He wrapped his hands around her waist, slamming against her with enough force to make the desk shake. Papers fluttered to the floor as he pressed her to the surface, running his hands along the slope of her waist to her hips as he hoisted her all the way onto the desk. She circled her thigh around his side while she ran a hand up and down his pecs, the scrape of her nails against his muscles the sort of sensation that traveled straight to his cock.

They kissed to a fast and furious beat, gasping for breath before diving back in again. The feel of her lips against his created a sinful surrender he couldn't get enough of. Sierra tugged his undershirt up, and he tossed it over his head to smack against the floor. Even though his erection strained the seam of his jeans, he'd keep himself in control. After dancing around this for so long, he needed some sort of satiation before he drove himself off the ledge.

"Enough of these," he murmured against her lips as he flicked open the button of her shorts. She shimmied out of them, and the heavy fabric dropped to the ground. The sight of her sitting on the desk—tank top rumpled with her lickable midriff exposed and a black, lacy thong the one thing keeping him from her—dosed him with lust. A growl started deep in his chest, the pounding intensifying as need overtook him. He sliced the sides of her panties with the edge of his claw and the delicate fabric floated off, exposing her drenched pussy.

He sank to his knees in front of her, Sierra watching his every move with her desire palpable in the air. The movement caused her thighs to tense in anticipation, and her pert tongue glided over her full lips. In one swift motion, he tugged her by the legs to the edge of the desk. She hooked her heels against his shoulders, and her knees bent as she exposed more of herself.

Dax leaned forward with a first tentative lick. She tensed her thighs at the motion, her heels digging into his traps. She tasted honey sweet, her nectar glistening as he began to lap at her pussy. Each stroke was slow enough to elicit a moan as he hyper-focused on the details, his erection growing thicker and heavier while he tasted the heaven between her legs. A moan came from her lips as he explored with feline patience, the cat satisfied by this brand of play.

"You bastard," she cursed when he flicked the tip of her clit with his tongue, finding a rhythm as he thrummed at the sensitive skin. Her hips bucked up as she ground her pussy against his mouth, her fingers gripping tightly around the edge of the desk.

"You've got a filthy mouth, Kanoska," Dax murmured before plunging his tongue inside her center.

She let out a loud cry before a "fuck you" slipped past her lips, causing him to smile. He returned to her clit, the quick motions of his tongue eliciting a reaction from her. The smooth skin of her thigh pressed against his cheek, and he broke from his attentions to bite the supple flesh. Her claws pricked out in response, digging a groove into the wooden desk she gripped.

"I'm going to make you come so hard you'll forget your name," he said as a smirk curled his lips. Dax trailed his tongue down her thigh, closer and closer to her core. Her legs quivered at the attention, and she tilted her hips up again in response.

"Stop fucking around," she swore, sweat beading her forehead. She bit her lip, digging her heels in even harder. He leaned in, gliding his tongue against her clit again and eliciting a jump from her. Dax began working her clit at a punishing rhythm, faster and faster, causing her thighs to tremble. The desk squeaked beneath them, and more papers fluttered to the floor as Sierra's cries exploded through the air. Her voice grew higher and louder, as if she didn't give a damn if the whole bar could hear.

Her legs quaked as she came, and her hips thrust toward his mouth as her entire body tightened and released like a wrung rag. She blinked, her eyes glowing with satisfaction, the sort that made him purr. He adjusted himself at the sight, his erection growing painful with need for a similar release.

"Holy hell, Williams," she murmured, running a hand through her sweat-soaked strands. "Where the hell did you learn how to do that?" Slowly, she sat up on the desk, even though her arms trembled a bit with the movement.

A mischievous smile crossed his lips. "Us feline folk are good with our tongues." His cock throbbed at the sight of her, hair tousled as she lay there, undone.

Her gaze traveled to the bulge in his pants, and her brow quirked up. "You don't think I'd leave you high and dry, do you?"

Dax scratched his nape, not wanting to reveal how badly he wanted her lips around his cock right then. "I'm good, sweetheart."

Sierra snorted as she slipped off the desk and onto her bare feet. "Like hell you are." She crossed the inches of space between them and snapped the button of his jeans open. Tilting her head up, she planted a slow and sensual kiss on his lips, full of lazy satisfaction as she unzipped his jeans. The thick fabric to pooled around the floor. Dax kicked them off behind him, turned on by the confidence of her movements. She gripped the elastic of his boxer-briefs.

His cock tested the tensile strength of the fabric, and as Sierra tugged them down, she slipped to her knees with wolfish agility. Her eyes gleamed amber and she licked her lips as her gaze glided up and down his cock. Dax's throat grew dry, witty responses abandoned in the wake of the hunger gripping him. He kicked off the boxer-briefs, his heart in his throat as she grinned up at him before tracing her finger down his length.

The contact jolted through him, causing his breath to hitch.

"Damnit, woman," he cursed. Sierra's secretive smile at the response was so goddamn hot he almost tossed reason out of the window to take her then and there. Except then she placed her lips around his cock, the wet heat of her mouth nearly making him lose his load. Dax let out a groan as he glided his fingers through her hair, tugging it into a fist.

His balls tightened in response as she curled her delicate fingers around his shaft. She began working his length with her mouth, moving with a sinuous smoothness guaranteed to push him to the edge. He'd been fantasizing about her for days, to the point his cock and balls ached. About the soft, full lips wrapped around his dick and the thick coil of hair between his fingers as he tilted his pelvis to fuck her mouth.

Her tongue stroked up and down his length as she moved in time with him. The hot suction of her mouth caused his thighs to tense, and hell, sparked his body to life as if he skated on the edge of a pool, ready to dive deep. His erection pulsed to the rhythm she created, the cycle he thrust his hips forward to as she sucked him down each time. Each time bringing him closer and closer to oblivion.

She twisted with the hand wrapped around his cock right as she descended again, the extra impetus sending him over the edge.

His fingers tightened in her hair as his balls squeezed. Ecstasy flooded through him with the crash of the tides and his cock kicked out as he came. Sierra kept her lips around his length, milking him for all he was worth as more cum spilled into her mouth. He floated sky high, euphoria crawling through his veins while his head spun from the rush. Finally, he stopped coming, and Sierra pulled back, wiping her forearm over her glistening lips before she swallowed.

He reached out and pulled her up by the hand, trying to mask the way his legs quaked in the aftershocks of his orgasm. Sierra had the same self-satisfied smirk on her face that he'd had minutes before, and Dax couldn't help himself. He brushed a finger under her chin as he planted a long and lingering kiss on her lips.

"Feeling a little calmer?" she asked, leaning against the desk again.

Dax snorted. "Mellow as anything. I'm ready to curl up and take a nap now. Don't mind if I purr."

Sierra shoved him in the side. "Ha, hilarious," she said drily, shooting him a look. "You have a celebration ready for you out there, so you better make an appearance. Your pack's been through a lot too. They need this as much as you do."

"You ruin everything," he muttered, fishing his underwear from the floor before he began sliding his clothes back on. "I'd be happy celebrating between the sheets, all night, if you catch my drift." He sneaked a glance at her. Despite the seriousness in her tone, a furtive smile clung to her face. He'd take his victories where he could get them.

"Sooner rather than later, we'll have to have the talk," Sierra said as she followed suit, slipping her jean shorts back on. She tossed her shredded thong into the wastebasket.

Dax shrugged. "I can last a while with this sort of fun, so take as long as you like, babe. I'm patient."

Sierra shot him a glare. "So, every time I speak to a guy, you're going to go rage-crazy and we'll have to address things? The only reason your hormones are brewing around there like a teenager is because this bond is unresolved."

Wickedness sparked in his smile. "If this is addressing things, I have to say, I'm not minding this scenario very much."

Sierra smacked his head before she sauntered to the door. She paused with her hand on the handle. "See you out there, big guy." She winked before she vanished into the kitchen.

Dax ran a hand through his sweat-soaked hair, his wifebeater now clinging to the film along his skin. Although his desire had been slaked for the time being, one taste was not enough.

Chapter Fifteen

A few days passed with one new challenger on the horizon who matched against Drew, not Dax. After the pipe-bomb incident, Sierra didn't trust herself to show up and watch without diving in to tear into the coward. Early morning sunlight filtered in through her blinds, deepening the colors of her tawny floorboards.

Despite all her efforts to the contrary, a certain mountain lion alpha worked his way into her thoughts to the point where she missed his pestering, and wanted to spend time with the bastard. And not just due to his clever tongue.

Sierra set her coffeemaker on percolate and the hiss of her machine emitted the scent of freshly ground beans. She tugged out her favorite mug, a mauve one heavy enough to knock someone unconscious. Slumping over the counter, she tried to wake up. With Drew tackling the next challenger, Dax had been spending his free time taking care of his pack in the Red Rock cabin, and she hadn't seen much of him.

Though that was probably a good thing. Guilt worked its way through her system, warring with the flutter of hope. So fast, she'd grown attached to him, even though the insistent pulse from her past begged her to run and never look back. Her fingers itched for a smoke as she brushed them over her empty jean pocket. She let out her breath in a steady stream, rerouting the motions into several uppercuts, slashing the air.

A knock sounded on her door.

Sierra snapped to attention, her hackles rising. The Red Rocks might know of this place, but they also knew better than to visit her here. However, one smartass wouldn't give a damn about bothering her.

Her heart sped up a couple of notches as she made her way to the door, claws out in case of an unwelcome intruder. Before she could turn the knob, the door flew open and Dax walked in.

Even with soot stains on his wifebeater and the edges of his plaid flannel frayed, the man looked good enough to take a bite of. The sunlight brought out several bronze streaks in his dark, tousled hair, and mischief sparked those blue eyes. A wisp of a grin hovered on his lips as it always did, as if any second he'd get into trouble. Not like the assessment stretched far from the truth. The man was a born pain in the ass.

He stopped a couple of steps into her place and sniffed the air. A smile spread on his face. "You make coffee for me?"

"No, but I'm assuming you'll be helping yourself anyway." Sierra rolled her eyes as she headed for her kitchen, trying to ignore the way her heart sped at the sight of him. If her traitorous body got this juiced after messing around with him, she was screwed if he ditched rather than completing the mating bond. That sort of loss she wouldn't be able to recover from—she'd be closed for business for good. She stepped up to the carafe filled with nectar of the gods. "Couldn't keep away, kitty cat?"

"Wanted to get my daily tongue-lashing from everyone's favorite pup alpha," he said, leaning against her countertop. "Plus, got word on Drew's round two. He won, so as long as I can tackle the next challenger, we should be facing off by the week's end."

Sierra pulled out a second mug and filled it to the brim. "Any word on that?" She offered over the cup, and Dax accepted, their hands brushing in the process. The electricity she'd chosen to ignore when they first met had grown undeniable now, raw in the air as if it had been painted there. Her gaze lingered on his lips as he took a sip from the steaming mug. His eyes glowed with amusement when their gazes met, and Sierra made quick work on grabbing her cup of coffee and fixing it up with cream and sugar.

"Looks like I'll be fighting Dominic Enrico, another pup alpha like yourself. Tomorrow at high noon, fitting for the cheesy western this is turning into." Dax blew on the surface of his coffee, shifting his jean-clad legs in a too-distracting way.

"He's dangerous," Sierra responded, the heat from the mug printing her palms. "Marine trained and deadly, combined with a lot of power for a shifter. The Yellow Rock pack has given us the runaround in the past, and we've almost come to butting heads. Every time, I managed to reroute to civil discourse, because I'm not sure that's a fight I could win."

"Lucky for you, I'm the one fighting him," Dax said with a wink as he polished off the rest of his coffee.

Sierra glared at him, positive her warning hadn't sunk home. "Now, quit dawdling. We've got places to be."

She crooked an eyebrow. "I think I'd know if I had somewhere to be. Pack-related activities are suspended while the Tribe's in town. My schedule has been freed up to watch you getting your sorry ass handed to you."

"Except for right now. Pop on your hiking boots," he said, his bossy tone making her want to slug him in the face. Sierra crossed her arms and didn't budge an inch. Dax heaved a sigh before giving her the side eye. "You're going to take off your shoes and plant, aren't you?"

She didn't resist the smug smile surfacing. "Not sure if I trust you yet, Mr. Williams. Not enough to go traipsing blindly after you."

He shook his head in disbelief. "I need to practice a couple of the moves you showed me the other day, and since you're a tough pup like this Enrico bastard, I volunteered you for the position. Getting a good hike in is just a bonus."

Warmth curled in her stomach at his words, even though she hid how his regard made her melt. He'd chosen to come to her for help, driving all the way out here to drag her along. The implied flattery was there—he trusted her strength.

"That so hard to say?" she asked as she sauntered over to her couch where her hiking boots had keeled over, leaving dried chunks of mud on the carpet. She laced them on and rose, wiping her hands on her jean shorts. Her canvas bag with spares lay rumpled on the floor, so she snagged it and looped it around her shoulder. Sierra caught Dax's eye as he leaned there against her kitchen counter. "Come on, you're holding us up."

Dax placed the mug on the countertop, his brows furrowed with annoyance. If he wanted to be a pain in her ass, she'd turn his own games around on him. "Anyone tell you that you're a stubborn, stubborn woman?"

"Every day of my life," she said, making her way to the door. Dax followed suit, slipping his hands into his pockets. Any hint of irritation disappeared from his easy smile.

Dax climbed into his beast of a truck he'd parked out front and leaned out the open window. "Hop on in," he called. Sierra basked in the sunlight as she made her way to the passenger's side.

Her heart floated more lightly than it had in years, as if the burden of being alpha had been lifted from her shoulders for a brief gasp. As she settled into the leather seat, she cast a glance his way. Dax leaned back, his powerful forearms taut as he gripped the steering wheel. Maybe because for the first time, she had an equal, a fellow alpha to confide in. He rolled out of her driveway, following the gravel road to the highway. The rays soaked his skin, highlighting the nick on his cheek and the dark stubble along his chin.

"You going to be there to cheer me along tomorrow?" Dax asked, his eyes twinkling. "Make sure to wear the whole pleated-skirt getup."

Sierra clenched her jaw tighter as the familiar prickle of irritation rose in her chest. "You had to ruin it all by opening your mouth," she drawled, running her hand through her hair to tame the strands tossed around by the breeze.

The sign for Ricketts Glen State Park appeared on the side of the road amid the tall grasses and surrounded by the thick, unkempt woods she'd run through too many times to count. Dax turned down the narrow dirt path leading deeper into the forest, the pines towering overhead. Already the sounds of the park pricked her hearing, the distant rush of the streams channeling into the dozens of waterfalls throughout this stretch and the whistling of birds chirping to one another from above.

They came to a halt in one of the parking lots where one or two other cars were stationed. Sierra hopped out of her side, her boots sending gravel and dust flying as she slammed to the ground.

"Race you to the first waterfall on the path?" Dax asked, his blues alight with mischief as he slammed the driver's-side door. Sierra's chest warmed. The sunlight, the loamy scent of earth, and the surrounding forest life dosed her veins with the best sort of high.

"You're on," she responded, setting into motion before the words left her lips. Dax barked a laugh, the sound rich in the air as Sierra hurtled for the embrace of the woods.

* * * *

"Even with the head start I kicked your ass." Dax crouched at the top of the trail winding around the waterfall, the churning water roaring in Sierra's ears. His cocky grin grew insufferable fast as his shoulders rose up and down in exertion. Sierra made her way to him, her breaths cycling faster from the speed of their run. They'd both mad-dashed up here in human form and lightness sank its claws in at the sheer joy of the way he played, a childish carefree way she hadn't embraced in longer than she could remember.

"Yeah, let's see how well you'd do in animal form," Sierra retorted, crouching to lean against one of the flat rocks alongside the path. She reached out to skim her fingers through the cascading water, the delicious chill sending a shiver down her spine. "Lazy cats don't win races."

"Apparently, neither do stubborn pups," he shot back, the wide grin on his face unrestrained. Unlike the coy smiles he passed when flirting, this one was raw and real, as if the sheer joy of the gorgeous summer day infected him as well.

Sierra couldn't resist taking advantage of the rare earnest moment from him. "How've you been faring through all this?"

Dax took a seat beside her on the ground with his long legs crooked as he leaned forward to rest his forearms on his knees. "I'm tired. Tired of the bullshit keeping me and mine from returning home. Tired of Drew still being a problem, and that there's even a chance the Cowardly Lion might snag both the territory and leadership of the Silver Springs pack smacks of bullshit."

Sierra nudged his calf with her boot. "That's not even a consideration, and you know it." Her voice came out in a near growl, filled with a conviction that stirred her soul. She understood his strain all too well, got how the sheer injustice could make this fight seem endless. If any morality were to prevail, Dax would win these fights and claim his pack. Unfortunately, she'd seen enough of life to know those hopes were as arbitrary as a summer storm.

"Better quit all this encouraging shit, Kanoska. Folks might start thinking you like me," he teased, nudging back with his leg. Even though his voice remained light, the weight of his gaze was anything but.

"You're not the worst," she muttered, her cheeks warming under his scrutiny. "I'll admit, I don't mind talking to someone who hates his brother as much as I hate mine. It's refreshing."

"I'm glad my family problems warm the cockles of your ice-cold heart," he drawled, his lips curled and his eyes dancing. Heat coursed through her. Beyond the tug from the mating bond, she had grown to genuinely like Dax Williams.

Gorgeous face and sexy body aside, the man was her equal, strong enough to respect, and despite the power games they played, her strength didn't make him back down or shy away. If anything, her stubborn resilience encouraged him to play dirty. Even with her shattered past and the damage sliced into her psyche, he didn't try to fix her or smooth over her jagged edges, just like she didn't try to convince him the relationship with Drew was one worth fixing. Both of them had learned early on your own blood could hurt the worst. That family was a choice.

"What will warm my heart is delivering your brother's head on a plate. He's caused so many problems for this region with this upheaval that you're no longer the only one who wants a bite out of him." She kicked a couple of stones around, sending one flying over the ledge of the waterfall. The fluid motion mesmerized her, a flow that sparked crystalline under the rays of the sun.

As she turned to look at him, Dax leaned forward, his fingers slipping through her hair as he cupped the back of her head.

He brushed his lips over hers, nothing like the fiery explosions that had erupted between them before. This gentle scrape of a kiss shocked her with adrenaline, coaxing the deep, burning core of her to the surface. The sun glowed along her skin, the warmth and light dizzying when combined with the sensations of his fingers tangled through her hair and his lips on hers. She melted into the kiss, embracing the heady swirl of euphoria that emerged as they continued this tentative exploration.

This wasn't some mind-scorching encounter where clothes hit the floor. No, this bordered on much more dangerous territory. The tenderness infused in his motions, the way her heart ached bittersweet, so overfull it grew painful. He left an indelible mark on her she never wanted to erase.

The scent of him, all cedar and sweat, had become a drug for her, the sort that traveled straight to her heart. Despite the resistance to the bond, they'd forged a connection most only dreamed about, one she'd never in a thousand years believed she'd find. His tongue slipped out, a caress against her own as Dax deepened the kiss. Every ounce of her begged to surrender and not just due to hormones running rampant.

Sierra pulled away, shattering the thick tension between them laced with the crisp scent of the falling water. "Tomorrow, after you fight Enrico, let's do this." She reached up to slip a strand of hair behind her ear. "I mean, if you're on board."

Dax crooked a brow at her, his gaze dancing with the spark of hope. "You're talking about the mating bond?"

Sierra met his gaze head on, refusing to hide her feelings any longer. "We've got something between us, and while I can't predict the future, I don't want to miss out on this."

He snorted. "Should I be surprised you're planning when we seal the deal?" Dax reached out to wrap an arm around her and tug her against him. Her heart stuttered in her chest, the admission between them filling her with a giddy zeal. "What's wrong with taking you here and now by the waterfall?" His voice grew husky with desire.

Sierra's gaze sparked, filled with the mischief he inspired in her. "Because you've got training to do for tomorrow." She hopped up, dusting her knees off before she reached down to grab her canvas bag. A smile stole her face, as bright as the glow she felt inside. "And if you're rolling around here, you'll never stand a chance at beating me to the next waterfall."

Before Dax could react, Sierra loosed like an arrow, plunging deeper into the woods.

He set off at once, kicking up dirt behind him. The woman loped up the stones of the narrow trail before them with the steadiness of a wolf, every step with that lupine agility. Dax watched her strides, marking them in his memory as he pursued, both man and cat thrilled at the way she played with him. Sweat pricked his brow, and the wind rippled the hairs along his arms as he raced after her.

Within minutes, she'd gone off the trail and out of sight.

"Sierra?" Dax called, slowing down for a heartbeat as he mopped his forehead with his shirt.

He caught the rustle of the nearby bushes too late.

Sierra lunged fist-first, hurtling toward him.

He lifted his hands to block her fists, dampening the force of the blow. His boots dug into the dirt as he staggered back a pace.

"You're fighting a wolf tomorrow," she said, her eyes gleaming with confidence. Her body moved with that same assuredness, one that made him burn for her all the more. "While you were able to rely on your speed with Dorlan, your next opponent will be faster. He might not have the forest for stealth, but he'll be unpredictable."

"Thanks for the heads-up, Yoda," he responded, stepping in closer. The moment he moved, she crouched on guard, ready for him. With her sort of vigilance, he wasn't going to get a blow in without her being able to absorb it. "What's your take on getting past that obnoxious guard of yours, then?" he asked, pacing around her as he waited for an opening to present itself.

Wolves might be vigilant, but cats were patient, and Dax had an incredibly long fuse.

She shrugged. "There're no guarantees in a fight. Every person is different. However, one thing that most folks underestimate is sacrifice. I'm not saying go and get yourself mauled." She pursed her lips, fixing him with a look. "However, everyone expects self-preservation to kick in. If you're backed into a corner, don't be scared to try something crazy. Better to risk than get killed."

Dax had been closing the distance between them, inch by inch, as she spoke. She'd been so wrapped up in her words, she hadn't noticed the gradual transition. He slipped his hands around her waist before she could throw another punch.

"Gotcha," he murmured in her ear as he drew her close. The spice of her scent, the heat of her body pressed against his, was enough to throw his senses into overdrive.

Sierra's lips curled in a sensual smirk that traveled straight to his cock, which ached at this point. The urge to tackle her and claim her rode him fiercely, but he had the perfect target for that pent-up frustration tomorrow morning at the match. The big bad wolf wouldn't know what hit him.

Chapter Sixteen

Dominic Enrico was one mean-looking sonofabitch.

Clouds darkened overhead, the air thick with the promise of a storm, but even without the clouds, Dax could've scented out the foreboding on the breeze a mile away. He stepped into the ring to face Enrico, a Latino guy who cast a mighty-long shadow and had more scars than teeth.

"Didn't realize I'd be fighting a bulldog," Dax called, unable to help himself in the shit-talking department. "Might want to wipe the bit of drool dripping from your scowl. I know I'm attractive, but I trust you can control yourself." A groan came from someone in the crowd, sounding all too similar to Sierra. He scuffed his boots along the ground, kicking up dirt around the clearing in the process. His heartbeat thudded a staccato beat at the impending fight and his lion paced in anticipation.

Another threat to his home and his people. Yet another fight that could result in the dissolution of the Silver Springs pack.

Enrico growled, but he didn't seem to have the reactionary anger of the bear clan alpha. This sort of bitter rage consumed a person until it thudded in their chest to the same tempo as a heartbeat. Which meant his favorite strategy of pissing the opponent off until they made a mistake wouldn't work. Sierra's warning resounded in his head—the worry had rung clear in her voice.

Dax glanced at the crowd. Most of the Silver Springs and Red Rock packs had shown up for this match, but his focus zeroed in on the lithe woman with her arms crossed and a scowl on those beautiful lips. Ever since yesterday, when they'd had their conversation, excitement twisted his chest, as if he prepared to dive off a cliff into the ocean. All he had to do was beat Enrico first.

Dax stretched his arms over his head, beginning to pace around the clearing in preparation for the fight. The midday sun shone without mercy, causing sweat to bead along his forehead.

Jess stepped into the ring, her presence like a lightning strike of focus. All the Tribe members had the sort of power that snared awareness at once.

She clapped her hands to get attention, though she didn't need to—the entire crowd had silenced the second she stepped into the ring. "You know the drill, boys. Animal forms for this fight. Dominic Enrico of the Yellow Rock pack and Dax Williams of the Silver Springs pack, you are to face one another in combat over this terrain once possessed by the Silver Spring shifters. The first one who doesn't rise, loses. The winner will advance to face the final combatant."

Her voice rang out through the quiet clearing and goose bumps trailed up Dax's arms. Like the last time, both of them stripped down and tossed their clothes to the edge of the ring. This was the sixth day, the final challenger keeping him from tearing his brother to pieces. He couldn't lose.

The air thickened with tension from the oncoming fight, from the onlooker's bated anticipation. Enrico's muscles tensed as the shifter readied to lunge, to fight, and to kill. His amber gaze glittered with menace, and a low growl emitted from his throat. Dax lifted his chin, meeting him head-on. This was his home, and he'd defend it with pride.

"Ready?" Jess called out, lifting her palms. The sunlight sparked through the trees, blinding him for a second. Dax sucked in a deep breath and let it flow through him to settle into his muscles.

"Fight," she shouted.

Once the word passed her lips, Dax transformed into the mountain lion, claws and fangs emerging as his body shifted until he crouched on all four paws. From across the clearing, Enrico shifted as fast. A hulking, obsidian wolf with a multitude of scars patched through the fur stood in the place of the Latino man. Before Dax could scope out his opponent's movements, Enrico struck.

The wolf tore across the clearing in several powerful strides, not hesitating for a breath as he loped toward him. Dax barely had the time to register the wolf, let alone where he was going to strike. Those razor claws glinted in the sunlight as Enrico reared up to swipe. Dax pivoted to the side on pure defense as the claws descended. The sharp points whizzed by him, slicing through tufts of fur. He lunged away from the wolf, his heart slamming.

Even as Dax backed away, Enrico didn't halt his relentless pursuit. The wolf moved fast and fluid, despite his size, with the same agility as Sierra. Dax couldn't exploit sloppy movements or lack of speed, nor could he wait for this guy to screw up with the dogged way he lunged into battle.

Another swipe. And another.

Dax dodged out of the way, unable to gauge anything beyond the immediacy of the claws flashing toward him. Fuck. Those amber eyes burned with tempered rage and the wolf lunged for him with immense strength and power. Dax didn't swerve this time, tumbling ahead with a flying leap to put more distance between them. He landed on his feet, feline grace turning his motions fluid as he whipped around to face his opponent.

The wolf charged for him again with speed and power to rival his own. Except he'd gotten pointers from Sierra, a wolf equally as stubborn, who possessed enough spirit to lay waste to an army. Enrico favored his back paws with the way he shot off them after each step, propelling him forward, faster. He dipped his muzzle in the direction he aimed, giving a micro-second of an indicator as to where he'd lash out.

Dax began his back-and-forth rhythm, ready to let the attacker closer this time so he could try to gauge a weakness. The wolf reared to the right, those claws glinting as his front paw twitched.

Dax pivoted to the left, circling around Enrico. However, the front paw never rose. Instead, Enrico slammed it down on the ground, using the force to spin around. Before Dax could dart out of the way, fangs glinted with the wolf's lunge. The tips sank into Dax's shoulders, pain exploding through him. He thrashed back and forth to toss the wolf off him. When the bastard pulled away, chunks of flesh went with him. The ache cramped Dax's stomach, hot waves rolling through at once. Blood pricked to the surface, pooling at the injury.

Fuck. He backed away from the wolf, his shoulder throbbing. Already, Enrico had scored a major blow and Dax hadn't even scratched the bastard. Letting that urgency overrule his senses wouldn't help, but he had to take an offensive role to stand a chance. Enrico bared teeth stained in Dax's blood as he stalked around, readying to launch into his next lunge.

No more trying to create distance. Dax didn't back away and instead focused on the shift of the wolf's paws and the tilt of his muzzle signaling the direction. Enrico sprang from his haunches, rocketing in Dax's direction. Instead of swerving out of the way, Dax held his ground, pounding a marching beat back and forth while his muscles tensed at the ready. He ignored the pulse in his shoulder and the flow of blood as droplets hit the dusty ground, instead honing all his attention on the attack.

The wolf's claws flashed, but Dax didn't budge. He swiped back, knocking the front leg out of the way.

Enrico swung again, the other side this time, but Dax remained steady, blocking the limb before those claws could land. Swipe after swipe, Dax deflected each one, staying afloat in the thick of the attack rather than seeking a way out. Each time he caught movement, he followed with a defensive tactic, over and over again. Shouts and hollers rang out from the captivated onlookers, familiar voices cheering for him. The support intensified his focus.

Enrico clenched his jaw, a red flag. As the wolf lunged for him, the jaws snapping like before, Dax surged to meet him. Right as those fangs threatened to descend, Dax smashed his muzzle along the side of the wolf's jaw, throwing as much force as he could manage into the blow. His own skull throbbed upon impact, but Enrico backed away, snapping.

Can't let the hit slide. If the wolf wanted to wear him down, Dax would be a storm.

He seized the opening, lunging for the wolf.

Forget a fight with claws—Dax's jaw widened as he descended, slicing through the short distance between them. His teeth sank into Enrico's throat and he latched on with all his might. Enrico thrashed back and forth, claws slicing into Dax's side, and still, he refused to let go. Deep gouges bloomed along Enrico's sides as he frenzied, desperate to get out of Dax's grip. However, he was just as capable of stubbornness, just as unwilling to budge.

Enrico slammed a limb against Dax's side, the force toppling him over. He lost the hold on the wolf's neck as they tumbled to the ground. Dax's vision hazed over, tunneling into fangs, fur and the blast of heat from Enrico's pungent breath hitting his face. Blood speckled on his face, gelling on his fur as he slashed, trying to combat the claws slicing his way. The dozens of cuts he'd received stung, creating a symphony of agony with every movement. He rolled on his back, at a disadvantage.

The wolf appeared over him, the head zooming too fast for Dax to block. His stomach convulsed as Enrico's head slammed home, straight into his throat. Dax gagged in response, lashing out with his claws. His throat pulsed with pain, the blow enough to make him wheeze with each breath. In the seconds Enrico pulled back, Dax dove for the advantage.

A brief space appeared between them, and Dax surged forward, aiming straight for the chest. Those amber eyes glanced down, anticipating the movement. Dax's heart thundered in his ears, and at the last minute, he switched tactics.

Right as Enrico descended with his claws sinking into Dax's already wounded shoulder, he twisted his head to the side, using the angle to lash up.

The tips hit flesh, sinking in.

An unearthly howl came from Enrico's shredded throat, one that sent shivers through him as Dax dragged down with his slice. Large gouges carved into those amber eyes, which squeezed shut in pain. Blood poured from the open wounds, the hot liquid splashing onto Dax's face. Even though his shoulder ached, he lunged ahead, executing the original trajectory of the blow. His head thudded into the solid chest, but with Enrico's eyes compromised, his reaction time slowed.

The movement destabilized the wolf's hold, and Dax slunk from under him, slipping out of the way. Each breath came out shakily, the wounds taking their toll. If Enrico landed another one, Dax was a goner. Couldn't give him the chance.

Enrico tried to whip around, but robbed of sight, his motions slowed. Dax raced for him at top speed, pushing himself faster and farther than before. He rammed into the wolf with enough power to send him flying. Dax skidded along the ground, kicking up dust as the force of the blow sent him sliding. Enrico didn't stand a chance at defense.

The wolf tumbled away, slamming to the ground with enough impetus to knock the wind from him.

Dax darted up to land on Enrico before he had the chance to rise. If he could win without killing, he would. He pressed the full weight of his body on the wolf, all paws evenly distributed to keep the wolf from budging. After several seconds of thrashing, Enrico stopped.

Dax glanced to the Tribe members, who rose. Jess crossed her arms while she waited.

A minute passed, but Enrico made no more movements to get up. Those seconds would be crucial to save his eyes and the wolf alpha understood that as well as Dax did.

Jess strode into the center of the clearing and began the count. Her voice boomed across the empty area, reaching the large crowd that had grown since Dax had last paid attention. Not like he focused on anyone but the woman who'd captured his heart. As Jess continued counting, Dax and Sierra's gazes met. Her lip trembled for a second even though her eyes blazed with steadiness. The sight lanced his heart.

"And one," Jess called, slicing her hands out with the motion. "Dax Williams of the Silver Springs pack is hereby declared the winner. Tomorrow at dawn, you'll be facing Drew Williams of the Silver Springs pack in the final challenge for leadership."

Dax stepped off Enrico. As he lumbered away toward the throngs of his Silver Springs pack, a gasp sounded from them, their eyes homed in on the battlegrounds. Dread pooled in his chest as tension thickened the air.

He whipped around in time to spot Enrico rushing for him, despite the damage to his eyes.

"Stop." Lucas's voice quaked through the air, a thunderous boom that drew everyone's attention. He lifted his hand.

Enrico made it a couple of steps farther before the gravel surrounding the ring rose in the air. Everyone froze, not only due to the shock of what they witnessed. Dax strained to even move a pinky, but his cat held him still, obeying the direct command of the Tribe member. The crowd remained similarly immobile, unable to break free from Lucas's order. Once Lucas's hand descended, all that gravel did as well.

Directly on top of Enrico.

Pebbles and stones pelted him in a fury, near burying him under the onslaught. Lucas watched, his eyes cold.

"That sort of cowardice will not be tolerated." His voice rang out before he nodded to the crowd to release everyone from the hold. Fear prickled across Dax's skin at the sheer power the Tribe wielded and the shamanic magic at their beck and call.

Members of Enrico's pack rushed past the crowd and into the clearing to dig their alpha out of the Tribe-made landslide. Even though Dax's wounds throbbed—the pain reaching a crescendo—once he slapped a bandage over his shoulder, he'd pull through fine. Not like he'd let a couple of scratches keep him from Sierra.

He hadn't forgotten for a second about her promise.

Screams and shouts pulsed through the air from his pack members, their eyes shining brightly with hope. His heart thundered in return, pride for his people surging with every step to them. The Tribe bristled with irritation at needing to get involved in the first place—the lot of them had little patience for lawbreakers.

Dax shifted back to two legs, fur dissolving from him as his body stretched taller and longer. Even in his human form, the lion claimed his territory as Dax shared the space when he was the beast. Blood trickled down his arms and legs, tickling as it slid along his torso to splash onto the ground while he walked.

He didn't think twice about his nudity until he caught sight of the way Sierra eyed him, and his blood heated in one fell swoop. The hunger in her eyes was a formidable thing, one that spread through his chest, heading south faster than he liked.

Kyle clapped a hand on his back as he passed, glancing down and letting out a whistle. Finn smirked as Dax sauntered past him, giving the guy a broad grin.

"Go get 'er," he said with a wink as he crossed his arms. Sierra cast a glance to Finn, the warning shot Dax expected from the stubborn woman. Too bad for Sierra, Dax planned on pissing her off in full. He'd had enough of dancing around the way he felt about her and how she sparked desires in him he'd abandoned a long time ago. The way she made him believe he was worth something—that he could lead his pack with pride.

He crossed the space between them and circled his hands around her waist before she could respond. Dax dipped down, his lips brushing against hers as the fires roared to life inside him. All the adrenaline, the raw pain and the intense longing for her melded together into one potent elixir. Sierra resisted at first, until she melted against him, her arms coming around his neck to draw him closer. Cheers and whistles sounded around them, but Dax ignored the crowd.

Right now, only Sierra existed in this space with him. From the moment he'd met her, she'd supported him, helping him grow and stand tall as a leader. Even the way she'd helped him train yesterday rather than delving into the desires riding him had been the edge of a blade difference that helped him win against Enrico.

Her lips were soft and lush even though how she kissed him was anything but. The pulse traveled southward as the way she pressed to him stoked his coals.

Dax pulled away, leaning to the side to whisper in her ear. "Let's get the hell out of here."

Sierra bit his earlobe, sending a sinful shudder through him. "Thought you'd never ask."

Dax didn't hesitate, reaching down to scoop her off her feet. She tightened her grip around his neck, a pert smile on her lips as she met his eyes. A broad grin claimed his face as his pulse thundered in anticipation of what would come. He nodded at the familiar faces of his pack and the Red Rocks before he carried Sierra to his truck. They'd skated around this bond for far too long. Dax was ready to lay claim to his mate.

Chapter Seventeen

Sierra leaned back in the leather couch that took up most of Dax's living room, listening to the spray of water as he washed up. Her nerves skated on edge, bristling from anticipation and the close calls Dax had earlier. Even though he'd beaten Enrico, the wolf shifter had brought him to a dangerous ledge.

Her throat tightened. Less than a week ago, his packmate, Lana, had stood over the body of her husband, Greg, pure grief and anguish rolling off her. How fast such an intense connection could be extinguished. If anything, the fight today strengthened Sierra's resolve in the choice they were about to make. Few were lucky enough to find their mate. She'd be a fool to throw the chance away when she could no longer deny the way he made her synapses fire. How at the end of a tough day, he was the one person she wanted in her space—the first man she'd brought back to her cottage.

The ceiling fans gave off a low snick-snick-snick as the amber light of late afternoon filtered through his open windows. Sweat beaded along her temple, and as the sound of the water shut off, she licked her dry lips.

The time of reckoning had arrived.

She ran a hand through her thick hair, remembering the last time she'd been on this couch with him when the mating bond first surfaced. In just two weeks, he'd become such an integral part of her life. When she was around Dax, she felt lighter, not as inundated by the responsibilities surrounding her. He made her laugh, pushed her to play and gave her space to open up while keeping her pride.

The bathroom door creaked open, drawing her gaze to him. In the dim light, shadows carved into every hollow, highlighting his defined abs marred by fresh scratches and old scars. He'd taped gauze over his shoulder, a patch from the wound earlier, which would already be healing. A towel slung around his waist, the strip of fabric barely covering his fine ass and the powerful thighs she'd witnessed in action when they'd sparred. She'd gotten her hands on that body when they fought, and she hadn't been disappointed in the slightest. The fighter utilized every square inch of his body, a weapon in its own right.

Rivulets of water clung to his lickable skin, drops sliding down the slope of his carved muscles. The room clouded with residual mist from his shower, though that wasn't the sole reason the air in the room grew hot and humid. The second their eyes met, her insides coiled tightly and she found it harder to breathe. Several strands of his wet hair plastered to his forehead, the rest splayed around messily, making her want to run her fingers through it. Mischief begged to play on his lips, a secret smile he shared with her.

"Took long enough," she called, not wanting to admit how the sight of him made her throat hitch, how the man was so gorgeous she lost her mind. "I thought you drowned in the mirror from staring into your reflection too long."

"Can't help it if I'm pretty," Dax said, a full smile blooming on his face. He crossed the room, each step deliberate as her gaze fastened on the barely there towel around his waist. She bit her lip as arousal wound in her core, an intense ache demanding satisfaction. "Let's cut the bullshit. You know you've been waiting for this as long as I have."

Sierra tapped the side of her chin, feigning innocence. "I came over here for a drink, Williams. I don't know what you've got percolating in your dirty mind."

Dax smiled as he stepped in front of her, the scent of soap and cedar like a drug to her senses. "I've got plenty of dirty things in mind when it comes to you, Kanoska." The husky way he said her name sent a shudder through her, and she couldn't help squeezing her thighs together. He leaned forward, gripping the couch beside her as mere inches separated them. Her clothes weighed too heavy, the layers too much when she just wanted to sink her claws into his tanned skin.

Each breath she took made her more aware of the heat between them, of the air tensing like the onset of a storm.

"You sure?" he asked, a flash of vulnerability in his gaze, the sort that broke her heart. This man had been considered second best his entire life. His family had discarded him, and even now, they tried to rob him of his worth. Even though he braced himself over her, one word and he'd walk away. But she didn't want that. Right now, she wanted Dax Williams, all of him.

"You're worth the risk," she murmured against his lips, the sensation sending a thrill through her. His blue eyes deepened to a stormy intensity at her words, his hand weaving through her hair. He leaned in to claim her lips with the sort of passion that traveled straight to her toes. The honeyed warmth and singular focus of the way he kissed, as if she was the sole thing in the universe worth a damn, gave her the answer she needed.

Sierra reached up to flick at the loose knot on the edge of his hips, sending the towel to the ground. His erection stood stark between his legs, the sight of it making her slick.

"I think you're at an unfair advantage," Dax responded, gliding up to brush his lips against her ear. He nipped her lobe, sending a shock of desire straight between her legs. She shifted, her thighs squeezing tightly as she tried to combat the fierce pulse inside her.

"Think you can level the playing field?" She arched a brow at him in challenge. A sensuous smile curled his lips, the sort that made her even wetter. He skated his fingers behind her back, brushing by as a click followed and her bra unclasped. Her nipples pebbled at the idea of those skillful fingers anywhere near her breasts. "Come on," she purred. "You can do better than a party trick."

His teeth gleamed with his smile as he lunged forward, biting down into her neck. The smooth movement elicited a moan before she could help herself. Her panties were already soaked, and he'd barely touched her. His scruff scraped against her neck, making it hard to forget the way the stubble had brushed more sensitive areas.

He slipped his hand under her tee until he cupped her breast, glazing his thumb over her rock-hard nipple. A spike of need drove through her at his touch, intensified when he leaned down to scrape his teeth over the tip through the fabric of her shirt. Another moan slipped past her lips as she tilted her hips forward, desperate to feel him inside her. She traced the scars of his chest, careful to avoid the patch of gauze on his shoulder. The raised skin of his war wounds mirrored the ones splayed across her back and along her thighs. Shifters might heal better and faster than humans, but they still carried their past on their skin.

Sierra traced down his pecs until she trailed her fingers along the velvet skin of his cock, the length of him stiffening to the touch. She wet her lips at the response, needing him to fill her in every sense of the word.

"Keep playing with that and I'm liable to blow, babe," Dax whispered, his hot breath tickling her ear. "I've been fantasizing about you from the day we met."

Longing surged inside her, a swell of want so fierce her heart threatened to burst. Because as much as they'd both tried to deny the way they felt, the connection had been there from the beginning, one that intensified with every interaction. He flicked open the button to her jean shorts and tore the zipper down. A second later they hit the floor. Right as his hands found the hem of her shirt, she slipped it off, tossing both her tee and the bra on the pile.

The hungry way he stared at her made her shiver, feeling exposed all of a sudden. Not like he hadn't seen every inch of her before, but that was pure animalistic lust. This—this depth she kept to herself for a long time, an attachment she hadn't allowed to form with anyone else because, time after time, they left. They all left.

She sucked in a harsh breath as she met his eyes. Her wolf gave her a nudge, her pinnacle of strength even now.

Dax broke the silence, understanding in his gaze. "I'm not going anywhere," he murmured, as if reading her mind. "You're the one I want, Sierra Kanoska."

She swallowed hard, unable to express the way her heart swelled to bursting, how she longed for him with a desperation which refused to be tamed. How she'd never believed she'd find someone who could slice her wide open the way he did, the sort of connection that filled her with incandescent joy.

Sierra wrapped her hands around his neck, brushing her lips against his as she tried to pour the maelstrom of emotions rushing through her into the kiss. Dax thrust her against the couch, pressing his erection against the thin fabric of her soaked panties. The heat emanating from his length made her writhe, her need sharpening to agony when she bucked against him. He groaned as he slipped two fingers past the elastic of her panties to glide along the seam of her and circle around her clit.

"You're so fucking wet for me," he murmured as he planted kisses along her neck, causing her back to arch in response. She crooked her knee as her heel dug into the leather sofa. Dax's nail grew into a claw, and he sliced through the underwear, sending the pieces fluttering to the ground.

"Are you going to destroy every pair I own?" she muttered, glancing at him.

His eyes danced with amusement. "I'm liking the sound of that. Next step is to get you to ditch the clothes entirely. Join me on the uncivilized side." His smile widened, creasing the nick in his cheek. Warmth flushed through at the memory of the way they'd sniped at each other the day they met.

A grin played on her lips, coming forth unbidden. "Are you going to talk me to death or fuck me?"

He slid against her again, his cock brushing across her slick pussy in a way that made her muscles tighten, that sharpened the ache inside her, desperate to be filled. Sierra tilted her hips, gliding up the length of him and causing a curse to erupt from his lips. The muscles of his neck grew taut as his eyes glowed, the lion in him emerging.

He nudged at her entrance with the head of his cock, and Sierra spread wider as her claws dug into his neck, skating the edge of animal and human. Even the slight push made her shudder, her sensitized skin reacting to the smallest motion. His obnoxious feline patience emerged as he inched in, taking his time as he stretched out her agony as much as possible. Sierra bucked her hips to take him farther, but the second she achieved her goal, he pulled back and begin torturing her all over again.

"I'm not sure which is stronger," she muttered, "the urge to fuck or murder you."

His smile whispered against her neck. "Stop trying to control the situation for once, and enjoy the ride," he murmured. Dax buried his teeth into the slope of her neck, the sharpness stinging her skin in a delicious way. She sank into the sensations threatening to consume her, at the scrape of his teeth, the heat of his smooth skin and the way he teased her with his cock, bringing her close to completion, only to steal the sensation away again. Her need to control was her final defense, which at last came tumbling down. He asked for her trust, so she'd give him her surrender.

As if he sensed the way she melted against him, he pushed himself in farther, rocking deeper into her. She let out a moan at how he filled her, rubbing her thighs against his as the sensation of their skin-to-skin contact sent a shudder of pleasure through her. Sierra leaned up to brush her lips against his, hungrily chasing his kiss to taste him again and again. His grip tightened along her hip, fingers sinking into the groove as if they belonged there.

Dax kissed her long and hard, the impact near stealing the breath from her. He plunged in the rest of the way, slamming straight into her G-spot, and hot waves of ecstasy rolled through her as she bucked forward to meet him. She blinked like a camera shutter, the flash sparking to life before her eyes as he thrust into her again to an undulating rhythm as natural as the tides.

They surged back and forth against the couch, and she ran her fingers through his damp hair and along his furnace-hot skin. She tasted the salt of his skin when she sucked at his neck, the mint of his toothpaste as their lips met again, all while he filled her to completion. The fullness of his length had her panting as sweat pricked on her brow, droplets rolling down her cheek, down the valley between her breasts. Each time they crashed together, the trail of curls around his cock brushed against her clit, sending a jolt through her that increased with the motion.

Sierra felt weightless, her body lost in myriad sensations, bliss overtaking any rational thought. She memorized the way his blue eyes darkened with need, the possessive way his palms wrapped around her waist, and the tender way he kissed her, a gentle scrape against her lips that she never would've placed with the smooth talker. Like this, he was so raw and real, bravado checked at the door in these moments together.

She twined her arms around his neck as she rode along with him, each collision bringing her closer to the edge. He increased the rhythm, moving faster and faster against her, the delicious friction sending a shudder down her spine.

He reached down, his fingertips rolling over her clit with a slick smoothness. Fire sparked through her veins as she sailed over the edge. Dax thrust deep, hitting her core as her muscles squeezed around him, and ecstasy radiated through her in waves. Heat spilled inside her as he came, his palms slamming on either side of her into the couch. They cycled ragged breaths, their sweat-slicked limbs tangled with each other as he leaned in to press a kiss against her lips. He shuddered as he continued to come, and she dug her heels into his ass, the leather couch sticking to her back.

Sierra sucked in a deep breath, dizzied from the sheer strength of the orgasm rocketing through her and her thighs quaking in the aftermath. She kissed him in return, reveling in the tenderness of his motions. He slumped against her, his weight pinning her to the couch. Sierra ran fingers through his hair while her heart surged with a wild churn of emotion.

As they tangled together on the couch, resolution flooded her veins, as if a key clicked open a lock inside her. The epiphany flushed through her in a radiant sweep, as if stepping into the sunlight after a lifetime in the dark.

Dax looked up, meeting her eyes as his shone with wonder. "Did you feel that?" he asked.

Sierra nodded. She couldn't explain it without sounding crazy, but a bond stretched between them, an unbreakable steel weave. Her mind opened and, as she scanned Dax, his every movement grew accessible as if the intense emotion pouring off him was her own. He pulled out of her, leaning against the arm of the couch before tugging her on top of him.

She rested her cheek on his chest, the heat radiating off their bodies enough to start an inferno. The closeness she felt with him was unparalleled, this rightness settling inside her. The distance she'd encountered with other lovers stretched out like a faraway memory when she lay here by his side. She could read Dax with ease, and she'd never been as comfortable in her own skin as she felt around him.

Dax grabbed her hand, lifting her fingers to brush his lips over them. The tenderness of the action seared her chest, and her heart ached with a mixture of relief and joy, as if she'd been searching for this completion her entire life to finally find what she'd been looking for.

"Just so you're aware, I don't share," Sierra said lightly, even though steel edged her words. "If we're mated, that means you're mine alone."

"That goes both ways," he murmured into her hair. "If any asshole tries encroaching on my territory, I've proved I know how to protect it."

Sierra snorted, glancing up to him. "You're assuming I don't slit the bastard from navel to throat first. I'm not a fainting idiot in need of protection."

Dax grinned, his eyes sparking with desire. "No way in hell a weakling would survive mated to me."

The thrill of the word pulsed through her with a finality that for once she didn't want to run from. She leaned forward to press her lips to his, exulting in the bond formed between them. A grin stole her as she murmured against his mouth. "So true—you're insufferable. I must be insane."

"Absolutely crazy," he said, flashing her a bright grin that caused her heart to squeeze tightly. "Ready for round two?"

Chapter Eighteen

Dax stretched out on his couch, wrapping his arm around Sierra, who leaned against him. As far as prep for the fight tomorrow could go, this was perfect. A flush decorated her cheeks, and the satisfied glow in her eyes made him brim with pride. He breathed in the scent of sweat and spice, uniquely her. His lion purred at ease, even though he'd welcomed a wolf to his bed. The way they'd come together left both man and animal feeling more complete than he had in his life.

Never in a thousand years had he believed he'd find someone like Sierra Kanoska. She shifted against him, her thick, silken hair pulled back into a bun, several strands glued to her forehead. He ran his fingertips along the raised skin of the scars on her thighs, the even slice of claws he recognized since he bore his fair share. She glanced at him, a glimpse of vulnerability in her eyes that made his heart squeeze tightly. He didn't need to ask to know these had to do with the brother she'd left behind, but her resilience and strength despite her trials made Dax respect her even more.

He'd spent his life being the discarded son, never measuring up by any standard, so he'd fucked around until for once in his life he'd truly wanted something—his position as alpha. And when even that chance had been stolen from him, he met Sierra, the woman and wolf who strengthened him during this, who took a chance when no other alpha would.

He leaned down to plant a kiss on her hair, eliciting a nose wrinkle from her even though she couldn't quite hide the hint of a smile clinging to her lips. His heart thundered with the realization this woman was his mate—that for once in his life he'd found a relationship he didn't want to run from.

In fact, ever since Drew had stolen the position Dax had fought for and splintered the pack, Dax found himself seeking out responsibility in a way he never had before. Tomorrow, he'd face his brother and claim his rightful place, but the hint of fear at being tied down no longer surged through his veins. No, with his mate by his side, he wanted to lead the Silver Springs pack into a new future—he wanted to stay.

His stomach rumbled, and he glanced to the door, willing the two pepperoni pizzas they'd ordered to arrive more quickly. With the way shifters ate, each of them could tackle a full pizza in a heartbeat and go back for more.

A buzzing sound came from Sierra's canvas bag, and she leaned down to swipe her phone out. Her brows furrowed as she stared at the screen and answered the call.

"What's up, Raven?" she asked as Dax trailed his fingers down her spine. She shot him a "not now" look, which made him want to antagonize her further. He pressed against her, growing hard at the feel of her velvet skin against his and the heat radiating off her lithe body.

Sierra froze, white-knuckling her phone. "I'll be over." He didn't miss the razor edge to her tone or the way her claws pricked out past her nails. The mating bond broadcasted her emotion loud and clear—stark horror that had him worried. The stony look in her eyes he'd seen before, the cold, calculating side of the alpha wolf that emerged in a true emergency.

"What happened?" he asked, already off the couch and slipping clothes on from his laundry bin. Sierra snagged her shorts and tugged her tee over her head in record time. Even as he buttoned his jeans, she'd slung the canvas bag over her shoulder and made a beeline for the door. He stumbled into his sneakers as he followed her, his keys jangling in his hand.

The sun had already set, since they'd spent the entire afternoon fucking across every surface in his house, yet even with the darkened skies, moisture still hung heavy in the air. He sucked in a mouthful as he headed straight for his truck. The urgency in the line between Sierra's brows and the way her hands kept clenching and unclenching delivered a hefty dose of fear. His ignition sparked to life, and the whitish-blue hue of his headlights sliced through the shadows.

The passenger door slammed shut as Sierra joined him. Her eyes gleamed with worry when their gazes met.

"Drew's attacking Beaver Tavern."

Dax didn't hesitate, peeling out of his driveway at top speed, their in-transit pizzas forgotten. Rage streaked through his veins like wildfire. The memory of how

Drew's attack on his compound had injured the families of his pack, and even severed some, still bled raw for him. He should've known. He should've figured his brother would pull some cowardly trick rather than meeting him on the battlefield tomorrow. As if he'd go running after Drew, threatened the lives of his mate's pack.

He clutched his steering wheel with a death grip, trying with all his might not to rip the thing from the rig. "We'll make him pay." Dax's voice came out in a low growl, the shared fear and rage in this car making the air grow thicker than the syrupy summer humidity. Sierra swallowed rather than responding, the woman collecting herself and trying to keep her impulses under control even though her eyes glowed amber.

Once the truck hit the smooth asphalt of the highway, Dax jammed on the gas pedal, the engine revving to life. The woods he'd grown up in flashed by as he soared across the highway toward their destination. Dax couldn't help the pang of regret piercing him.

Back in the days when he used to run through those woods with his brother, he never would've believed they'd come to this. That the fight for leadership after their dad's death would get this drawn out and dirty. Even if they only shared a mother, they had been brothers in every other sense of the word throughout the years. Now, he was dealing with an entirely different person.

"I'm so sorry." The words slipped out from him, the guilt rising in his throat like gorge. "If I hadn't come to you for help, your pack wouldn't have gotten mixed up in all of this."

Sierra blazed with calm fury despite her initial reaction, iron control an innate part of her when she assumed command. “Do you think us so weak we’d shrink from a challenge?” she asked, brimming with confidence. “We chose to help you, and my pack stands by their choices. You didn’t bring this hell on us, your brother did, so don’t waste your time on regret.”

Dax nodded, humbled by the unerring focus of his mate. If he could be a fraction of the alpha she was, he’d consider himself a success. Even in the face of her home being threatened and one of her pack’s gathering places under siege, she managed to pull herself together to lead. His heart brimmed with pride. Out of anyone, she’d chosen him as a mate, and he’d do everything in his power to honor the decision.

Farther down the highway, the homey lights of the Beaver Tavern stood out, a beacon in the distance. The sight had become a salve to his displacement since his brother took over their homelands, and already Dax had built memories with Sierra here he never wanted to erase. His lion paced in his chest, anxious to release, to tear into his brother and claim the vengeance his cells screamed for. The closer he got to Beaver Tavern, the more dread infiltrated.

Orange and gold lit the area, and not from the lights.

Flames licked at the surrounding trees, and trucks and cars were parked haphazardly in the gravel lot, the spotlight illuminating the clash of not only humans, but mountain lions against wolves. Beaver Tavern’s door lay open, and based on the way people raced in and out, the inside brimmed with a similar state of chaos.

Anger roared through him, sparked by the sight of the destruction his brother wrought. He screeched to a halt at the turnoff into the lot.

“Don’t go gunning for the center of the chaos,” Sierra barked out, her voice taking on the harsh growl of her wolf side. "Pull off to the side, and if you spot your brother's car, that's where you need to be."

Dax gripped the steering wheel tightly and guided his truck into the narrow gap leading to the empty side of the parking lot. His brother had had the same Cadillac for years, one he'd taken as a personal challenge to keep running. Dax would recognize the black car with the myriad slapped-together parts anywhere. The second he skidded to a halt on the gravel, Sierra dove out of the passenger's side.

She immediately began shifting into her wolf form, and by the time she hit the ground, she landed on all four paws. Her clothes hit the ground in shreds. She didn't communicate where she headed, but he didn't need to ask—she'd be running to the heart of all the chaos inside Beaver Tavern. His heart squeezed tightly as he quelled the urge to follow. Working as a team sometimes meant working apart, and although the desire to protect her coiled within him, she was tough and smart enough to handle herself.

Dax turned the engine off and hopped out of his car, remaining in human form. His boots hit the gravel, spraying stones everywhere. Feet away, the trees licked with flames, a forest fire that could spread fast. They had to get a team on that at once.

Sierra loped in through the entrance of Beaver Tavern, the silver wolf disappearing into the building. A second later, a wolf howl rent the air, the eerie, ear-piercing wail drawing every eye in that direction. The noise contained all the mourning for the surrounding destruction, all the rage at the unjust attack and all the ferocity of the fight they would bring. Dax understood the howl for what it was though—Sierra sounding her rallying cry.

At the alert of her howl, wolves entangled with former members of his pack separated, leaving them to rush the inside of Beaver Tavern. One by one, the members of Red Rock pack rallied to heed the order of their alpha.

Dax scanned the crowd. If Sierra was heading for the center of the action, he'd be her eyes and ears. He hadn't spotted his brother yet, but he recognized some of the faces and the lions fighting down below, joined by strangers from neither pack. He swallowed hard, knowing what his next course of action had to be. Despite the need for revenge pounding through his veins, he knew this had been an act of desperation. Drew was scared.

Dax had almost beaten his brother before, and this time, no one could jump in to break up the fight. If Drew lost tomorrow, he'd lose everything—his position, his land and his supporters. Despite those who followed him, Drew would remain as emotionally isolated as he'd always been, trying to seize things through cowardly and bullying tactics like Dad had. Dax hadn't chosen that route. The people who followed him had the sort of loyalty that leaders would kill for, and he'd made an alliance forged in steel, forged in the mating bond between him and Sierra.

Unlike his brother, Dax wasn't desperate. And because of the strength his pack and the Red Rocks lent him, he could see the big picture for once.

"Pack," Dax called, his voice booming over the growls and hisses lighting the air. "Quit fighting. The fire will spread if we don't stop it."

A screech resounded through the air as a black Cadillac pulled out from a parking spot. Dax caught sight of the man behind the wheel as he veered past him, the first glimpse he'd gotten of his brother since the day they'd fought for the alpha position.

His brother had always been the handsomer of the two with the sort of blond-haired, blue-eyed surfer thing most girls lost their shit over. The fights must've sapped his energy, though, because dark circles intensified the blue in his eyes, and a long scratch marred his cheek, one that would heal ugly. The man who'd led the rogue Silver Springs into this fray was taking the cowardly way out yet again, abandoning his people to fend for themselves.

All the jealousy Dax had stored over the years of the favoritism his father had showered over his brother dissolved in an instant. In that simple glimpse, the man transformed from an equal to fight against into a coward he pitied. He didn't envy the lonely path his brother had chosen. Dax could waste his time chasing vengeance, but tomorrow, he had the chance to exact justice—far more important. Here and now, they had to salvage what they could of Beaver Tavern and help those who had been injured.

Several trees whined as the fire ripped through them, bringing branches crashing down and fueling the inferno.

The Cadillac's tires screeched as his brother peeled onto the highway and raced away. At the sight of their leader departing, several of the rebels broke away from their fights, shifting to two feet as they rushed to their cars. Rylie and a couple of others stayed, vicious snarls erupting from their throats as they poured unrestrained rage into attacking folks once considered family. To Dax's relief, he hadn't spotted Uncle Aiden in the crowd. Before his pack could pursue, Dax called to them again.

"Throw dirt on the fire to smother it. Those closer to the tavern, run in and get buckets of water." His voice echoed through the clearing. If the fire managed to spread, not only could the blaze take down the forest, but it would smother Beaver Tavern as well, trapping whoever remained inside—including his mate. Orders delivered, Dax didn't wait any longer as he rushed toward the crackling blaze in the woods.

Chapter Nineteen

The state of the Beaver Tavern broke Sierra's heart. She couldn't help the mournful howl that ripped from her throat.

Those bastards had used human weapons again, blasting bullets through the wooden floors, the walls and the ceilings. The windows splintered into shards along the ground. Blood splattered the walls, dribbled across the floors and streaked the overturned tables. Bile rose in her throat at the tinny scent, at the blood of her packmates splayed all over their gathering place. Rage swelled with the fury of a storm, containing no words and no lofty statements to rally behind. It was the deep bellows of wrath inspired by the raw grief suspended in the thickened air.

Soft sobs came from behind the bar and growls from the back room. Sierra's head spun with a toxic spell of sorrow and anger, of the choking, blinding need for vengeance against the massacre to her home. Her breaths came out heavy even as she forced herself to focus, padding across the splintered hardwood and kicking past the spent shells of the machine guns that had been brought into her tavern.

Focus. One thing at a time.

Sierra tried to ignore the broken windows that once lit up like home from the highway and the bashed-in pool table she'd spent so many nights around with the others, laughing and tossing back a couple of pints. She slipped around the bar to the quiet sounds of whoever waited behind there. The sight socked her in the gut.

Raven sat on the floor, tears streaming and her phone glowing forgotten on the floor. She clung to the still body of Seamus, streaks of blood coating her arms and soaking into her shirt. Bullet holes littered his chest, as if they'd pierced through the bar, the wounds raw, red and oozing. Her packmate lay there unmoving, his mouth agape, so different from the easy smile he wielded when he operated behind the bar. Sierra's stomach tightened, and a whine came from her throat, drawing Raven's attention.

One of mine. The bastard murdered one of my pack.

Raven blinked at her, those dark eyes glossy with tears. "He jumped in front," she murmured, forcing the words out. "They were aiming at me…" Raven trailed off, a sob rising in her throat again. Agony painted Raven's face, the same that pierced right through Sierra. At the loss of the vibrant smile, the teasing words and the fierce protection of Seamus. She'd no longer see him behind the bar, one of the hardest working employees in the place. He wouldn't be pouring her a pint on a bad day anymore or cracking a bad pun that made her groan. Those wise, expressive eyes had closed for good.

Sierra padded to Raven and swiped her muzzle along the woman's cheek, doing her best to brush away the tears. The hot splash of them tickled her nose and another whine slipped from her throat. The grief reached her wolf just as keenly. Raven tilted her head in submission as Sierra tapped again against her cheek. Her heart squeezed tightly. This destruction should've never happened—her pack had no chance at an honorable fight. The attack went against shifter law, broke the rules and the code engraved on her bones.

The room dizzied around her, and even though growls and snarls came from the back room, her paws stayed. She didn't want to move from this place. She didn't want to leave Raven alone with her sorrow right now, to leave Seamus lying there surrounded by a pool of his own blood.

The overwhelming scent of blood and the surrounding chaos resurrected memories of the bombs set among Dax's people. She'd told him to stand tall—that his people needed him to lead in that moment more than anything—and as alpha of the Red Rock pack, she needed to do the same.

Sierra tilted her muzzle in Raven's direction before forcing herself away from the scene. Away from the guilt threatening to devour her. Her packmate lay dead on the floor, part of the family she had chosen stolen from her. This entire nightmare had happened because she'd taken in the Silver Springs. Because she'd been fucking around with Dax while her people were being attacked. Sierra raced toward the snarls coming from the back room, shutting out the poison that threatened to take over her brain. Down that spiral lay madness.

She slunk into the kitchen right as a dish went whizzing by her head to crack against the wall beside her. Shards of porcelain sailed through the air, and she swerved to avoid the shrapnel. Finn fumbled for another plate on the opposite side of the room. A mountain lion Sierra didn't recognize squared off with a russet wolf she definitely did. Jer lunged forward, jaws snapping at his opponent while Finn wielded another plate, ready to hurl it. His gaze skated up to meet hers.

"Sorry, boss," he called out, his voice thick with the rage consuming them like a wildfire. The way his gaze darkened, the guilt had ensnared him—she didn't need to clarify what the apology was for. No one else would be hurt, not on her watch. A male lion stalked back and forth, ducking right out of Jer's way. Too bad for the Silver Springs traitor she'd sparred with their kind before, and Dax's level of combat prowess blew this asshole out of the water.

Sierra let out a snarl, drawing both the lion and Jer's attention her way. Jer's eyes flashed as his gaze met hers, and she leaped in, fangs bared as she hurled herself toward their enemy. The mountain lion's attention swung her way as he reared in defense. That would cost him.

Jer seized advantage of the distraction, jumping onto the mountain lion with a flurry of claws and fangs. He reverted focus too late, as Sierra crashed into the fray on the other side. Her claws sank into flesh, tearing up fur and flaying the skin in the process. The mountain lion didn't stand a chance against the alpha of the Red Rock pack. Within seconds, he shifted into his human form, the movement blurred in the midst of their transition.

Jer lunged again, but Sierra stepped in the middle as the bloodied male bolted out of their grip, hightailing for the back door leading to the woods. Finn tossed another plate. Even as the porcelain shattered, shards slicing into the Silver Springs male, he didn't stop. A curse flew from his throat before he leaped out the open door.

Sierra shifted to two feet before stalking over to the office, which remained untouched despite the spray of blood and shattered dishes decorating the black-and-white tile of the kitchen floor. She snagged a spare cotton tee and gym shorts from the closet, slipped them on and grabbed another pair before she returned to Jer and Finn. Jeremiah shifted to his human form, his muzzle mutating into his face. The second his hands reformed, she tossed him the set of spares. Finn snarled, his teeth baring as his wolf lunged to the forefront, begging the transition.

She shook her head, her chest heavy. Tonight felt a lot like defeat however she spelled it. Those bastards had laid siege to her home and destroyed the place she'd inherited from the former alpha of this pack. Already they'd lost Seamus, and who knew how many other Red Rocks had been injured or worse?

"Why'd you stop me?" Jer shouted, his voice echoing through the kitchen as his teeth elongated into the fangs of his wolf.

Sierra turned to face him, rage taking a bow under the weight of the loss they'd suffered. "Drew and his people are desperate, and they're scared, because tomorrow is the day of their reckoning. Because our people have suffered enough tonight, and I refuse to lose another one of you due to revenge. Tomorrow, Dax will win and the Tribe will deliver their punishment."

"Yeah, boss, but what if he doesn't?" Finn asked, his voice solemn as a cemetery. Sierra's throat tightened.

She didn't want to broach a future where Dax lost, or worse, where he didn't survive. The thought sliced her heart with agony, the sort that turned every breath painful.

Sierra lifted her chin, refusing to let those fears overtake her. Not now, when her people needed her. "If he doesn't, we'll search them out and slaughter every last one of those bastards. Now, let's send them off our land, so we won't lose any more of our own tonight."

Finn nodded and strode toward the opened door exiting to the forest. He grabbed tightly to the doorframe before turning around to meet her eyes. "I'll handle any remainders here. Go to them. Your people need you right now."

Sierra nodded at her beta, who vanished through the door. She placed a hand on Jeremy's shoulder. "Help Raven with Seamus. She's still shell-shocked and could use the assist right now." Her hand pressed over her mouth with the realization. A bitter curse ripped from her throat. "Fuck, we'll need to let his sister know. Once the chaos calms, I'll give her a call."

Her eyes burned, but she swallowed the grief, keeping the tears at bay. "We can start cleaning this place up."

Jer nodded, running a bloodstained hand through his curls, unaware of the streak he left. Sierra sucked in a breath and stepped past him, making her way through the wreckage of Beaver Tavern. Even though Raven's gaze bored into her as she walked by, she trained her focus front and center. If she stopped to look at Seamus lying there on the floor, at the friend she'd lost tonight, she'd crumble.

And right now, she needed to stay strong. Her pack needed their alpha.

The moment she stepped outside, the scent of smoke stole her attention. Most of the cars had cleared out and she didn't spot any of the mountain lions or the couple of coyotes and bears scuffling with her wolves. Drew might have been behind the attacks, but between the Tribe's concern over the pipe bombs and these strange shifters here tonight, he didn't seem to be their only enemy.

Sierra strode in the direction of the trees, her heart in her throat. In her haste to get inside and take care of the tavern, she'd forgotten about the blaze in the trees, one that could have spread to engulf the bar just as fast. Despite the smoke pouring into the night sky to smother the stars, the trees no longer burned, and only a couple of licks of flame ran through the clearing.

Red Rocks and Silver Springs worked seamlessly together. Those in human form had formed a bucket brigade, while wolves and mountain lions kicked dirt to snuff out some of the flames. Dax wove amid the crowd, barking commands, diving into the tasks and overseeing the whole operation. Her mate had picked up her slack with no direction necessary, stepping back to see the big picture when she had rushed in to help her people.

Her chest loosened with the relief she needed after the events of the night. Dax caught sight of her and nodded, his mouth forming a grim line. She nodded back, not needing to say a word to communicate her gratitude. In such a short time they'd woven deeply into each other's lives. It should've terrified her—closeness with anyone in the past had sent her scrambling—but no longer.

Dax was her mate, her partner in every sense of the word, and after years of shouldering the burden of leadership alone, she'd found someone she trusted enough to share the weight.

As the packs stamped out the last of the fire, Dax waved them over. She stood in front of the Beaver Tavern, beckoning the Red Rocks to her side. Sierra ran a hand through her hair, her fingers growing slick with sweat. Her breath came out sharp from her tight chest, the horrors of the night one that would live in her memory for a long time. Blood streaked the fur of too many of the approaching wolves and mountain lions, and more than a couple of those in human form limped.

"Drew and his rebels have escaped tonight," she called out, her voice carrying across the clearing. Even as Sierra stood there facing the dozens of weary gazes, she shut off the intense boil of emotions threatening to overflow as she operated on autopilot. A couple of curses broke out and several of her wolves moved back and forth on padded feet, searching for something to lunge into, to take a bite out of.

Sierra lifted her chin, her hands balling into fists. "That doesn't mean he will escape justice. Red Rocks, this bastard has come here and destroyed our home, unprovoked and unwarranted. This coward doesn't fight by our rules. Silver Springs, he has divided your people, turned against your rightful alpha and torn friends and family apart."

Dax watched from the back of the crowd with his arms crossed. Even from here, guilt tugged at his frown, his stance defensive. And he wasn't the only one. The mountain lions in the crowd kept their heads bowed with their gazes skating the ground and those of the Silver Spring in human form wouldn't look up either. Shame coated each and every face, shame that sparked outrage in Sierra.

"I was planning on waiting with this news," she started, meeting Dax's gaze across the crowd. His brows lifted in surprise—of course, he anticipated where she headed with this. "However, after what we experienced here tonight, together, this is important now. Dax and I are mated."

More than a couple of jaws dropped and Finn shook his head with a smug half smile. The shock rolling through the crowd drew their attention, snapping the Silver Springs pack out of their self-loathing. Sierra seized on the opportunity.

"Our packs are connected in a unique way, and tonight, more than ever, you can be proud of how you banded together. Of how you helped one another against a common enemy and how we acted to protect, not destroy. Tonight we'll lick our wounds, and we'll start to mend what we can. However, tomorrow when Dax steps up to challenge his brother, we will stand united again, our alliance forged in the fights we shared and in the blood we shed."

At the mention of his name, Dax wove past the others to stand by her side. He squeezed her hand and she didn't shy away. In this light, leaning on him didn't make her weaker—this sort of togetherness made packs strong. The connection was how they remained whole during the tough times. The two alphas faced their packs in a show of solidarity in the wake of the tragedy Drew caused, one that wouldn't be allowed to go unpunished any longer.

The Red Rocks lifted their heads in a howl followed by the hollers and growls of the Silver Springs, their packs uniting once again. The air reverberated with the power of the individuals standing before her, people she was proud to call her pack and allies and a man she was proud to call her mate.

As the sound began to die down, Sierra waved toward Beaver Tavern, gathering everyone's attention. "Those injured, gather in front of the tavern. Ella, Gene and anyone else with training in first aid, join them. To the rest of you, we've got to make sure the fire's entirely stifled before we rest up for the morning. Beaver Tavern might've taken a beating, but we haven't been snuffed out. She'll rise up better than ever in no time at all."

Seamus's corpse lay inside and that alone would make this a long, grueling night, but Sierra led the way to her tavern, determination settling in her veins. Time to get to work.

Chapter Twenty

Thunderstorms didn't hold a candle to the intensity that charged the clearing.

The Tribe members glanced between the two groups standing on opposite sides with mild interest. Not like they interfered, though—unless Dax and Sierra brought an official report regarding last night to them, they wouldn't get involved. And no way in hell would Dax stretch this limbo out longer than necessary. He'd settle this dispute with Drew on the testing grounds here and now.

Dax paced along the worn earth he'd spilled blood on yesterday. Many of the cowards who'd attacked last night hadn't dared to show their faces today, which meant Drew's side consisted of a handful of scowling folks Dax had once considered pack. Some wounds didn't heal easily. Between the pipe bomb attacks and shooting up Beaver Tavern last night, they'd cemented themselves in enemy territory from here on out.

Meanwhile, the attack last night had rallied everyone under his and Sierra's watch, so the force he had at his back to support him today was inspiring. These fighters were resilient, resourceful and loyal—traits he hoped to emulate and honor on this testing ground.

A rumble came from the black Caddy pulling into the parking lot. Dax stopped pacing and sucked in a deep breath as he straightened to greet his opponent. Drew slipped out of his car, aviators on and his wrinkle-free tee begging for some bloodstains. Dax's brother tugged off the sunglasses and squinted as he tossed them back into his car before sauntering over. Dax didn't miss how he looped around, veering as far as possible from the Red Rock pack and Dax's supporters.

Several growls lit the air at Drew's appearance, the air heating more fiercely than the sun could swing. The slight hunch in his brother's shoulders as he jogged over was telltale. He knew he'd done them wrong last night. The silver hue of the clouds rolling in stained the area with shadows, but already the sticky humidity clung to Dax's skin like paint.

Even amid the loam of the earth and the tingle of fresh greenery, Dax caught the spice of Sierra's scent from the crowd. She'd been in his bed when he had gotten up at a more reasonable time than her preference of dawn, and he couldn't imagine a better way to wake up. With his one-nighters he'd been out the door before they ever blinked twice in the morning. But back then, he'd been insecure, directionless. Now, he knew where he was meant to be. Win or lose, he'd face Drew today with uncompromised honor.

Drew stepped into the clearing, drawing the rest of the crowd's attention. The sight of his brother on this familiar territory smacked Dax with déjà vu. Six months ago, he'd stepped into this ring as a nobody within the pack—few folks thought he stood a chance against his father's favorite. Yet that day had marked the beginning of a new chapter.

The death of his father had been the lifting of a veil. Dax wouldn't spin his wheels fighting authority—at last he had a real opportunity for change, a chance to take the Silver Springs pack in a better direction.

His brother scowled, the ugly gash down his cheek marring those picture-perfect features—the broad jaw, wide, easy smile and arched nose Dax had never inherited from their father. Except now he understood the reason why. Navi stepped past the other Tribe members, her arms crossed and her brows furrowed while glancing between the two of them as if she watched a ping-pong match. She sucked in a breath and sauntered toward them, her exaggerated steps like some old cowboy in a Western heading to a duel.

Gravity descended between him and Drew as if with the onset of a storm. Dax straightened his stance, sliding his thumbs through his belt loops.

"You must be shitting yourself right now," Dax called out, drawing his brother's attention. "Didn't think I'd make it this far, did you? I'm a stubborn bastard—too stubborn to back away from this fight. Maybe I did inherit some Williams traits after all."

Drew snorted, the derisive sound causing his skin to prickle with irritation. "You're not a Williams, but you are a bastard. Why Dad wasted his time raising an ungrateful wretch who wasn't his blood is beyond me. Promises to our whore mother only stretch so far."

Dax rocked back and forth where he stood, not batting an eye. Based on the way Drew's lips pursed, he was waiting for some shock and awe, but Dax had spread the word to his pack once he found out. And as for those who sided with Drew—well, they were assholes following a dead guy who didn't deserve their loyalty.

"What a relief," he called, "to find out I wasn't related to that monster. Dad won't save you now though. You're going to pay for your crimes, not only against our pack, but against the Red Rocks. And right here and now it's you and me—no cheats, sneak attacks or bombs."

Navi's lips twisted in a scowl at the statement, but what or whomever the Tribe investigated around town, they'd remained silent and evasive on the subject. "You two reached the final round, but since your fight as shifters for alpha was interrupted, you won't be fighting as mountain lions, but as humans. The winner will become alpha of the Silver Springs pack and preside over the contested territory. No weapons, no claws and no fangs."

Dax frowned. After all the fights in his lion form, he hadn't expected that one. Not as if he'd grown rusty on hand-to-hand. Sierra left nothing to chance, and he had welcomed every opportunity to get hot and sweaty in their human forms. Drew scowled at the announcement and those familiar blues flashed at him, flickering with fear. His brother rolled his shoulders, a fake smile on his lips. Dax would know, since that was where he'd learned the technique first.

Regret sliced him, a piercing ache in his chest as he met his brother's gaze. Beneath all the ugliness marring their relationship, he couldn't erase those early memories. Of roughhousing as cubs until Uncle Aiden had to split them apart and laughing as they dove back in for more. Of following Drew through the secret paths in their woods, because his big brother knew all the best spots to hide from the adults. Of the way Drew had gotten him a birthday present every year, even if Dad "forgot."

However, he also couldn't dismiss his brother's actions. Beyond breaking the Silver Springs pack in two, the pipe bombs and the attack last night had drawn a line in the sand past the point of forgiveness.

Dax glanced behind him, at the familiar faces in the crowd who'd arrived to support him. Kyle, Marcy and Rick and even Ally-cat had managed to make it out, though she leaned on a pair of crutches. Finn and Raven stood side by side, stony-faced and resolute as they watched him from afar. And Sierra's gaze remained level, her determination unshakeable, and her faith in him a power unto itself. She gave him a slight tilt of her head in acknowledgment. She believed in him, enough to rest justice for her pack on his shoulders.

He wouldn't let her down.

"Fight until one of you doesn't rise," Navi called out, her tone a shade bored. The Tribe had witnessed dozens of these matches, including the ones this week. For those guys, this spelled the end of an annoyance. She lifted her hands. "Ready, and…go."

The sudden declaration jolted Dax to action. His muscles tensed, and he dropped into a fighting stance, shifting side to side.

As the words left her lips, Navi's arms dropped and she jogged off the arena to join the rest of the Tribe by the lawn chairs. Dax began circling the same way he would in lion form, the urge to stalk his prey one that remained. Except he'd had this fight a thousand times over with his brother. His father had taught them to ram ahead similar to the fighting style of Dominic Enrico. Dax didn't often follow his father's directions, but Drew did.

Despite the cowardly way his brother had attacked last night, his gaze sharpened and his body buzzed with the alert aura of a fighter. Drew might be an asshole, but Dax had fought his brother enough to know he was a dangerous asshole. And today, after the violence his pack and the Red Rocks had suffered, he couldn't afford to lose.

Drew circled in a similar fashion, but Dax didn't take the bait to leap in half-cocked. Instead he waited, and he paced. His head buzzed with the adrenaline rushing through his veins, and his lion walked with him every step, as present as if he'd shifted. The air thickened enough to drink it down and the faint stench of blood marred these grounds from the countless fights witnessed here throughout the years.

Drew's right hand twitched.

In this fight, speed meant everything. Dax couldn't take the defensive. His shoulder still throbbed from the other day and if his brother applied pressure on the weak spot, he'd crumble.

Dax leaped ahead, racing toward his brother before he could get the jump on him. The breeze swept strands of his hair back as he snapped in with the precision of an arrow loosed from a bow. Drew's fist whipped around, but Dax had seen the motion coming. He swerved around the swing, grabbing his brother's arm and yanking him forward. Propelled by the motion, Drew staggered, making the mistake of showing his back.

Dax's elbow slammed down on his spine with a crunch, the blow reverberating up his arm.

A groan flew from his brother's lips, but the man darted ahead, rolling against the ground to slide out of the way. Drew kicked up clouds of dust with his movement, and Dax quickstepped to the side, avoiding the roiling grit.

Before his brother could rise, Dax ducked low, aiming a sweeping kick for the legs.

His boot thudded against Drew's shin, but his brother clamped his hands around his ankle, tugging him farther. Dax followed the movement. Air whirred around him, and drops of sweat slithered down his back as the midday sun pounded onto them. He launched onto his brother with the ferocity of a lion, his claws begging to come out and play. With a crash, he collided against Drew, the full weight of him slamming into his brother's side. Drew's grip around his ankle loosened.

If his brother wanted relentless, that was what he'd be.

Drew drove his fist an inch above his head, a near hit.

Dax didn't back down. Instead he rammed his head forward, his thick-as-fuck skull slamming into the asshole's ribcage. Bones creaked, but he didn't know whose as he led with his right shoulder to slam Drew back. He thudded against his brother so hard the breath nearly flew from him, and Drew wavered, teetering back and forth as he tried to find his balance.

Can't stop there.

Before Drew righted himself, Dax wove in with an elbow again, a forearm thrust that sent him tumbling.

The second Drew landed on his back, Dax struck. He leaped on top, pinning his brother, leading with his arm across his chest and sinking in his weight to follow. Drew's fist clipped his cheekbone with a resounding thud and Dax bit back the tang of blood, sliding to the side to avoid the oncoming punch from the opposite side. His brother's spit flew to smack against his cheek, but Dax shoved his body down to keep the asshole pinned. Peripheral sounds turned into a distant buzz compared to the sharp intake of breath, the groan of muscles and the crunch of bone.

Drew wanted an easy fight, but their father wasn't here to hand him a leg up. Here, he had to face Dax in his full fury.

Here, he'd pay for the lives he'd stolen.

For Greg, whom Dax had found lying dead in his own home.

For Seamus, who'd been shot while defending his pack.

Drew's knee dug into his stomach as he used the advantage to pivot. The tap to his chest distracted him long enough for his brother to roll out from under him. Before Dax could follow up, Drew rammed full force into his wounded shoulder. Pain thundered through him, the gash on his shoulder throbbing with newfound intensity. Bile rose in his throat. He bit back a curse and staggered out of Drew's radius.

Desperation drove his brother, though, and before Dax could whip his head up, Drew's fist drilled into his chin. Dax's head snapped back, the sound echoing through the clearing as his brain blanked for a heartbeat. Even as his balance shifted beneath him, he pivoted in loops rather than staggering as he circled out of Drew's reach.

A cocky grin rolled onto his brother's face as he approached, the skulking posture and the hunch of his shoulders brimming with confidence. Asshole had sussed out his weak spot, so that'd be his target from here on out. Wetness spread along Dax's shoulder, blood leaking through the fabric of his shirt.

Fuck.

Drew thrust his knee up, and Dax surged forward in response, ready to greet the blow. At the last second, he stopped mid-stride.

Left shoulder.

The fist came sailing in his direction right as the knee retreated.

Dax ducked.

His hands shot up, one wrapping around the asshole's forearm. He curled his other hand into a fist before it crashed against the side of Drew's elbow. His brother let out a piercing howl, but Dax wasn't done yet. With the joint destabilized, he tugged the forearm the opposite way.

The crunch echoed through the air as bones snapped.

Drew slammed his head into Dax's already shredded shoulder before he collapsed to the ground, a low growl reverberating through his chest.

When the blow landed, Dax's stomach revolted. Nausea rushed through him in a sickening sweep, enough to make him stagger and his surroundings swirl. The vertigo claiming him spelled bad news. If he didn't end this soon, the pain would make him black out. He'd lose by proxy.

A loud howl came from behind him, one he'd recognize anywhere, sending goosebumps up his arms. The piercing sound sliced through the haze of pain in his mind until he reached the clarity he'd been searching for. She believed in him—for Sierra, for the Silver Spring pack, he would fight. He would win.

Drew pulled himself up to face him with his left shoulder slumped from his injured elbow.

All or nothing.

Dax's jaw tensed as he clenched his hands into fists. Keeping both shoulders back so he didn't give himself away, he launched toward Drew, closing the distance between them. Drew twisted to the right, shielding his injury. Dax didn't have that luxury. Either he pulled this off or his brother would bring him to his knees.

The wind whistled past him, drying the sweat across his forehead, and his vision tunneled to the sight in front of him. To his brother's defensive stance as Drew prepared to ram him head-on. Pristine clarity descended, the sort where the entire world slowed around him, where each second stretched and his even breaths cycled in his ear. Where the sun pulsed on him and he sucked in the thick air, drinking the humidity laden with the greenery of his home.

Dax sank into the purity of the moment, his walk across a razor blade.

He baited with his shoulder and his brother jumped for it, his right arm soaring for the open wound.

An inch away, Dax pivoted around until he swung to Drew's left side.

His fist snapped out, as fast as a quick draw. And with Drew's wounded elbow, Drew never stood a chance.

Dax slammed his knuckles into his brother's temple with force that reverberated up his arm. His brother's head twisted to the side, drops of blood and spit flying through the air. Drew rocked back and forth on his feet for a half second.

Until he dropped like a stone.

Drew hit the ground with a smack, enough to draw gasps from the crowd. Dax crouched, ready to defend as he watched the still form of his brother, the slight rise and fall of his back a sign the man continued to breathe. Tense seconds passed as sweat crawled down Dax's cheek, tickling as it dripped to stain his shirt. His heart pounded in his ears and his shoulders heaved with each harsh breath, sending another wave of pain radiating through him with every pull.

Navi's footsteps drew his attention as she stepped into the clearing, the crowd so silent each step echoed like rolling thunder. Dax glanced at Drew, who lay there unmoving, and he swallowed, his throat so dry it caught.

Navi stopped in the middle of the clearing, her direct gaze landing on him. "Dax Williams, I hereby declare you the winner. You are the rightful alpha of the Silver Springs pack." Her eyes softened and a gentle smile lit the fierce woman's face. "Congratulations."

As he turned to greet his pack, the clamor of their roars, howls and cheers nearly knocked him off his feet.

Chapter Twenty-One

Sierra stepped up to the cabin on the opposite side of the lake, a two-story beauty with a glossy wooden exterior that blended with the surrounding pines. Dax's boots scuffed the ground as he approached beside her. His wounded shoulder had been cleaned and rebandaged, but the second he'd slipped away, he'd wanted to come here. The other members of the Silver Springs pack pulled into the sprawling parking lot, the screech of tires and rumble of trucks over gravel echoing through the air.

"I haven't been back here since they drove me out," he said, placing his hands on her shoulders as he pressed up behind her. She leaned into him, basking in his cedar scent, one that dizzied her mind with memories of the way they'd crashed together yesterday. If she had her way, they'd be repeating that tango many, many times tonight.

Sierra leaned up to brush her lips against his as Dax deepened the kiss. The tender touch sparked adrenaline in her veins, the sort that made her breath hitch.

"Stop making out," Finn called, striding up behind them. "We've got a hell of a lot of drinking to catch up on. Hope this joint is stocked."

Sierra pulled away from Dax, turning to face her beta. A smirk lit Finn's face even as she fixed him with a glare.

Dax snorted. "If my brother was in charge, I can guarantee they'll have booze on hand." He grabbed her hand, tugging her toward the front door.

Kyle jogged from the opposite side of the cabin, his cheeks flushed. "Boss, there's a keg out back. Should we tap it?"

"Like I said." Dax gave Sierra the side-eye. He stood tall as he turned to Kyle, dominance in his stance that hadn't been as strong before. "Grab a couple of the others and get the keg prepped. We've got a lot to celebrate, but respects need to be paid as well." The orders came naturally, and, she had to admit, the role of alpha looked good on Dax Williams. Kyle tossed off an easy salute before launching into a jog back to the keg.

Sierra squeezed his hand. "You're right. Our packs will need to blow off steam tonight." The loss of Seamus remained fresh among her packmates, a still-bleeding wound, and Dax hadn't gotten over the death of his friend Greg. Until now, he hadn't had the luxury of mourning. They might be celebrating Dax's victory tonight, but they'd also be honoring those who'd fallen.

A beat-up old sedan pulled into the lot and a familiar, pint-sized member of the Tribe stepped out. Navi's cocoa skin gleamed with golden tones under the sunlight and her thick hair glistened with a couple of coppery strands amid the chestnut brown. She strode over to them, as both Sierra and Dax straightened on reflex. Finn hung around with his arms crossed while he gave Navi the full eye-scan. Sierra shot him a dark look—she knew her beta well enough to gauge his interest. Finn shrugged, running a hand along his buzz cut.

"Come to visit li'l ole me?" Dax drawled as Navi approached. "I'm honored." Sierra resisted the urge to deck her new mate. He reached out and grabbed Sierra's hand, flashing her a mind-melting smile that managed to quell her temper and send her mind to dirty, dirty places.

Navi shook her head, a brass smile on her face. "Don't flatter yourself, Williams. You lot should've reported Drew's attack last night to us at once. Aiden Hannigan from the other Silver Springs pack stepped up and told us everything. Cleanup is going to be a pain in my ass. When Drew wakes, he's going to have more than a blistering headache to deal with. The crimes he committed will guarantee the lowlife's locked up for a long time. And if he happened to collaborate with the owners of those pipe bombs, he'll be in for a different sort of hell."

"Good," Sierra growled, unable to stave off the venom in her voice. The monster had been a thorn in her side from the moment she heard his name. Dax stilled as he dipped his head in response, but she caught the shadow lingering in those blues. She squeezed his hand, offering a small smile. The earnest one he gave when their eyes met sent slow warmth rolling through her like honey. No matter what road bumps they faced, she'd chosen this man as her mate, and quiet, small moments like these renewed her faith in their decision.

Dax let out a breath, running his hand through his hair. "Apparently Uncle Aiden's not completely hopeless," he said. "So are you going to keep acting all mysterious about the threat in our region? As alphas, we should be in the know." Dax's gaze rested on Navi.

She pursed her full lips, hazel eyes sharpening. "All you folks need to know is if you hear word of the Landsliders, report immediately to me. And if you happen to encounter Mackey Kendricks? Run." At that, she hooked her thumbs through the loops in her cargo pants, averting her eyes. "What are you going to do with the other rebels?" She rolled back and forth on the balls of her feet, obviously done disclosing information.

Dax heaved a sigh. "Different problem for a different day." Marcy and Rick strolled by, their three kids in tow. The oldest girl locked gazes with Sierra before giving her a tentative salute. Sierra returned the gesture with a fierce smile, the warmth nearly bursting inside her chest. The front door creaked as the family stepped inside, followed by Raven and Jeremy close behind.

"Well, I'm sticking around the area to deal with our other mess," Navi said with a sigh. "So you better be plying me with a lot of alcohol tonight if I'm to stomach this country-bumpkin territory for much longer."

Finn stepped up, looping an arm around her shoulder. "Let's go raid their liquor cabinet."

Navi crooked a brow with an incredulous look directed at Sierra's beta but shrugged as the two of them stepped off in the direction of the Silver Spring cabin.

Sierra glanced over, realizing her hand remained in Dax's. She tugged forward, stepping on her toes to plant a kiss on his lips. The taste of him sent her reeling, the heat that sparked through her body like fireworks at the touch. Comfort, relief and a deep, unrelenting warmth claimed her chest, her heart overfull with adoration for this man. Even if she wanted to punch him half the time. He placed his hands on her cheeks, drawing her toward him as he deepened the kiss in a way that made her toes curl.

With a sigh, he pulled back. "You ready to join me in there, oh mate of mine?" His eyes met hers and behind the teasing, dancing flicker in them, she caught the gravity of his question.

"I've got no idea how we'll handle being mated and running two packs, but we've already overcome a hell of a lot to get here," she said, her voice sobering as emotion threatened to overwhelm. Her eyes stung at the sheer thought of the boundaries they'd crossed, the way they'd fought together and supported each other through this entire trial. "We'll probably clash a little—well, maybe a lot. But stubbornness goes both ways, because I hold on like hell to those I've claimed and you're mine."

"Likewise, babe," he responded, his voice husky. "Whatever comes our way, we've got the support of allied packs and an unshakeable bond. I think we'll pull through." He squeezed her hand, guiding her toward the door. "You know, our packs aren't the only ones who need to let loose tonight." A dangerous glint lit his eyes, the one that stole her heart from the start. "I've got a couple of ideas in mind, several involving you up against a wall."

Sierra shoved his good shoulder, rolling her eyes even though she didn't bother to hide her grin. "Down, boy. Let's start with a drink." She reached out to grab his hand, her touch hunger satiated as, hand-in-hand, they headed for the door. When Dax Williams had entered Beaver Tavern, she never would've imagined she'd end up with the cocky smartass. However, she'd watched his resilience through this whole ordeal and how he'd risen to the occasion, stronger every time.

Pride thrummed through her veins as she followed her mate inside his pack's reclaimed home filled with Silver Springs and Red Rocks united. Her relationship with Dax was worth fighting for, a desire and contentment she never dreamed possible. Somehow, they'd created a bond between them deeper than the one she'd formed with her pack. With Dax, her mate, she'd found a love that could endure.

Want to see more from this author? Here's a taster for you to enjoy!

Tribal Spirits: Forged Decisions

Katherine McIntyre

Excerpt

Finn had been avoiding Beaver Tavern all week.

He sat in his Challenger, tapping ash out of the window as he stared down Raven's car in the parking lot. Sneaking around, hiding from her at every chance—he was being pure chickenshit right now. The Tavern had already flicked on the open sign for the day and ever since the night of Dax's victory when he'd spent the night with Navi, he hadn't wanted to face Raven. Hadn't wanted to untangle the complicated whatever they'd been dancing around all these years. His wolf lunged inside him, demanding straightforwardness he couldn't muster right now.

He let out a stream of smoke, glancing at the time on his car's interface. With his next class in a half-hour, he didn't have long enough to dive into a serious conversation with her. His throat tightened when he wheeled the car out of the lot and his tires crunched over gravel. Even as he made the justifications in his mind, he knew he hid behind excuse after excuse.

A better man would've never strung Raven along this long, knowing at the end of the day they would never have a future together.

Finn wasn't a better man—hell, he wasn't even a good man most days. The previous alpha had groomed Sierra to take the reins and not him for a reason, despite their matched skills and strength. The current alpha of the Red Rock pack maintained the unshakable moral code his people needed to hold their territory and form a united front against any challengers that might come their way. Finn threw out a whole lot of swagger, but time and time again, he crumbled.

The hickory and oak trees of Rickett's Glen rolled by, the dense forests he'd grown up running through. Those trails beckoned to his wolf on a regular basis since he skated a little more on the wild than the others, a little too attuned to the demands of his other side. He drove this route to work daily on the way to his studio. Thank everything holy he'd carved a successful niche teaching kickboxing and MMA out here, because if he hadn't found some outlet for his aggression, he'd be flipping tables and slinging punches every night.

After the way he'd wussed out of the discussion with Raven yet again, he needed to burn some of the nerves making him buzz. Which made the upcoming class he was teaching perfect timing.

He pulled up in front of his studio, Kelly's Gym, and parked along the patch of beaten earth that constituted the parking lot. Finn approached the shoebox of a place he couldn't have been prouder of, the plaster siding glowing white and the near-flat black roof within jumping distance. His place might not compare to the massive gyms in cities like Philly, but he'd thrown a lot of work over the years into turning what used to be a couple of sessions a week into a thriving business.

He loped up the steps and unlocked the door, the light stuttering on once he flipped the switch. The pale white walls of his gym interior needed a new paint job, since every imperfection glared brighter against the red and black mats lining the floor and the six drop-down punching bags. The sets of weights lining the back were stacked neatly in place—folks might call him anal retentive, but he shouldered a fair amount of personal pride in this place, which he wanted to represent as a clean, organized space.

Finn strode to the back and set the big fans on, his sole means to combat the sticky heat rolling through this sector during late summer. Once strong breezes gusted through the room, he began his own set of warm-ups, his wolf snapping at the reins a little more than normal. Not like he thought he'd be less agitated in charge—Sierra made an amazing alpha—but ever since he'd become beta of the pack, a restlessness had kept him on edge.

Even with their old alpha, his wolf had lunged forward to strike at any chance, a rebellious side of him that clashed with the community he needed to survive. Wolves were pack creatures and he'd witnessed life outside their circle early on when his shithead folks decided to ditch. The time away had been a nightmare.

Drops of sweat beaded Finn's brow as he worked his reps with the punching bag, burning some of the aggression heating his chest. One-two, one-two, one-two.

A slight creak from the opposite side of the room startled the hell out of him. Finn whipped around, droplets flying from his arms when he turned toward the door he'd never heard open.

"Don't stop for my sake—I was enjoying the show," Navi drawled, leaning against one of the pillars in the center of the room. The damn panther could sneak around better than most, even with the raw, lethal energy radiating from her. Like Finn needed more of a knockout punch—the sight of her shoved the air from him. Navi's hooded gaze, those deep hazel eyes screamed sex, and the casual smirk on her full lips was a private one she'd only shared since the other night.

The tank top and running shorts she wore left her rich brown skin on full display, highlighting the sort of hips he wouldn't have expected on a pipsqueak like her. Not that he'd ever call her that—he might be a dumbass sometimes, but he valued his life. She was one of the Tribe, the shifters imbued with the great spirits of the animals they transformed into and the governing force of their kind.

When he'd started flirting with the scary-as-fuck Tribe member during Dax's trials, he knew he was playing with fire, but he expected her to shut him down. Never in a thousand years had he anticipated their unforgettable night.

Man and wolf alike couldn't help the way his cock throbbed at the mere sight of her. When she moved, he noticed, and when she entered a room, he felt her presence as loudly as if she screamed in his ear.

"Got some aggression to burn before class, soldier?" she asked, approaching with a balanced, feline grace to her movements. His heartbeat raced. He wanted to slam her against the mats to claim every inch of her luscious body, but she patted the side of the punching bag. "We've tried that route," she purred, her eyes glinting with amusement. "Now let's see how you fight."

Inches separated them and Finn stepped closer, moving into her space. "How's that a fair fight, pussycat? You've got all those spirit-gifted tricks to whip out."

Navi didn't back down an inch, her calm smile twisting into a smirk. "Like I need my abilities to bring you to your knees. Quit making excuses, Finn Kelly, and spar with me."

His heart thumped in his ears, the blood pumping through his veins in an intoxicating way. A slow grin rolled onto his face as he stepped back a pace and sank into a crouch. "I suppose we've got enough time for one round. Don't go crying to your buddies that a Red Rock kicked your ass."

Her mouth quirked with her grin, but Navi emanated lethal calm, her eyes flashing the silver of her panther even though she remained in human form. She was out of his league in every way, her abilities and the magic at her command the stuff of whispered legends, and yet Finn couldn't help trying to catch the tornado by the tail. As she circled around him, the movement slow and seductive, her power crashed down like a tidal wave over the room until Finn near drowned in it.

Too bad he was a stubborn fucker.

He bared his teeth, fangs forming while he watched her with a wolf's vigilance. A cat like her could play and tease forever—he knew without a doubt between the two of them, she'd hold out longer. He rolled his shoulders, the urge to lash out prickling through him. Thankfully, he'd never refined an attack style relying on patience. Finn had been throwing punches before he ever learned to speak, and teaching for a long time—long enough to see a thousand types of styles and figure out how to combat them.

She watched his every movement, waiting for him to tip off his first strike—which meant he needed to employ either speed, or a feint.

Maybe both.

Finn tilted his right shoulder forward to test the waters and tossed a few one-two punches in her direction. Navi's palm blocked one and her forearm deflected the other.

Would she take the bait?

The micro-second twitch of her knee gave him the hint.

Right when she tried to thrust her knee into the opening, Finn pivoted out of the way. He grabbed her closest arm and tugged, throwing her hips off balance, and before she could right herself, he stepped in close and personal. With the opposite forearm, he slammed into her stomach. To his surprise, she didn't stumble, just toed a few paces in the sort of dance anyone skilled enough could muster.

Inches away, he didn't stand a chance of avoiding her punch.

The blow slammed into his stomach, and only the quickstep away helped diminish the force. This close, he could smell the vanilla scent of her skin, could see the way her forearms tensed into corded muscle, honed for lethality like his own. Her gaze flashed, giving him the one heads-up of where she would move to next.

Her hips pivoted as she unleashed a kick.

Instead of running, Finn surged forward, square in the center where the knee hit. Before her leg thudded against his body, he'd already tackled her. Navi wouldn't appreciate him holding back and he'd learned to use his muscle and heft to his advantage. Even as her thighs tensed and she tried to shove him, he sank like a stone overtop her. Together, they crashed to the ground.

He landed on top with his forearm pressed over her chest. She tilted her hip to the side, but he refused to move his weight. "Check," he said, a grin stealing his lips as her eyes blazed.

Her leg slipped between his thighs a second later. The moment he felt the movement coming, he rolled to the side. If she nailed him in the nuts, he'd be incapacitated.

Navi pounced, taking the foreground when she tackled him. The elbow she drove into his chest stung like a motherfucker, but he couldn't help the smile that appeared on his face. The dogged persistence she fought him with reminded him of his bouts with Sierra and the way Navi analyzed on the fly never failed to impress him. She was the sort of fight that wasn't just about proving something—right now, they were having fun.

He shoved her off again and she rolled into a crouch, rising at the same time as him. Her wicked grin mirrored his own as her shoulders heaved up and down from their form of play. She circled again, a predatory spark in her eyes. Finn's heart raced, sweat trickling down his forehead. Hell on earth, he was so alive while he tracked her movements, ready to dive in again.

"Getting tired already?" he taunted, rolling his shoulders as he prepared for another lunge.

"Tired of listening to you jaw off, Kelly," she retorted, even though her eyes sparked with amusement.

This time she took the initiative.

Her sneaker ground against the floor with a squeak when she launched through the air toward him. His instinct begged him to throw his hands out and catch her, following with another tackle—but instincts lied and she was clever.

Instead of lashing out, Navi tilted her right shoulder forward, making no effort to guard her body.

Finn barely got his arms up in defense as she slammed into him full force, using her body like a bludgeoning weapon. Despite her small size, she grounded herself like a powerhouse. Finn staggered back, the blow throwing him off kilter.

Except she didn't stop there.

Navi lashed out with her fists, needling two quick jabs into his open spots.

Instead of falling back or losing his balance, Finn danced on his feet since he kept his body loose to absorb the blows. They stung something fierce, but Navi wasn't throwing her full weight into them. Which meant she was planning something else. Her hip twitched to the right.

Finn thrust his arms down. The moment her leg snapped out, his hands wrapped around it. The side-sweep she attempted halted when he used his steadied stance to shove her leg out. Before she could regain her position, he pushed her forward, sending her tipping back. Finn's heart pounded, a grin stole over his face and sweat trickled down his neck, his shoulders. He leapt forward to tackle her to the ground.

She threw a jab straight to his gut, enough to make his stomach squeeze. However, he refused to relent and crashed onto her with his full weight. They tumbled to the ground again.

Her chest pulsed beneath him, her sweat-slicked limbs tangled with his. Their eyes met, a wild wickedness in Navi's that sent his mind to dirty, dirty places, reminding him of all the other things he'd like to do to her pinned to these mats.

The door to his studio creaked, drawing his attention at once.

"Am I interrupting something?" Kyle asked. The Silver Springs shifter scratched the back of his neck while he tried to avert his stare.

Finn hopped off Navi, but before he could offer a hand up, she rolled to her feet.

"Just your trainer getting his ass thrashed," she called as she made her way to the far wall lined with towels. She wiped away the thick strands of her pixie cut that had plastered to her forehead. He followed her over there, already covered in a sticky film of sweat he wanted to shower off, a combination of exertion and the August heat spreading through this place.

Finn snorted. "Kyle, get started on your basic stretches—we'll get rolling in a minute."

"Want to walk me to my car?" Navi asked, phrasing it less as a question and more as a demand. While the woman possessed a confident sexiness, she didn't do subtle for shit. Honestly, he liked that about her at once—Finn had been on the receiving end of so many mixed messages and sent some of his own, enough that he wanted a clean break from that sort of mess.

"Sure thing, sweetheart," he said, slinging his towel around his neck. Her eyebrows lifted at the term, one Sierra would've smacked him in the face for, but, for some reason, every time he pushed with Navi, she tolerated his cocky bullshit. Like she could see right through every ounce of bravado he flung her way. The mats squished under his tread while Finn and Navi made their way across his gym, out into the blazing heat.

When he stepped under the glaring sun, his skin heated in response, begging to soak in the rays and turn his olive skin three shades darker. Navi's old Plymouth sat out in the parking lot, the paint peeling and more than a couple of dents on the exterior. Finn's fingers itched to grab his toolkit and fix the sedan as best he could. Sierra had once told him he 'mother henned' over his Challenger with the amount of attention he poured into keeping his girl running smoothly.

"So, I'm guessing you didn't show up to tangle around on the mats with me," he said, leaning against her car, the metallic body creaking from his weight.

"Color me surprised, Sherlock," she drawled. "Didn't think you had a brain behind the pretty face." She leaned against the car beside him, her proximity comfortable.

"To be fair, you're as blunt as a sledgehammer," he responded, tugging at his wifebeater, which had glued to his chest.

"I'm not familiar with this area, and I'm going to need help from someone who knows every inch of this terrain. Sierra recommended you, but I needed to get a grip on your fighting style, because what I'm going to ask you isn't short on danger." Navi gave him a serious look that was all Tribe, pride and regality emanating from her. So different from the expressive woman who'd melted for him in the bedroom.

His skin prickled at the idea of danger and his wolf pounded approval in his chest. He'd been straining at the seams following orders here—even the normal responsibilities didn't appeal to him since he'd seen Sierra inundated with resolving the stupidest conflicts, and as her beta, he wasn't needed for much. He wanted to be in the thick of doing something useful and had honed his body into a weapon begging to be aimed and used.

"Sign me up," he responded, his tone firm.

Navi crossed her arms over her chest. "Don't even want to know what we're up against?"

Finn shrugged. "I trust you're not going to throw me into a suicide mission—you think I've got a pretty face." Navi's gaze bored into him at the comment, but those full lips quirked with a smile. When he'd first met the hardass, intimidating Tribe member, he never would've thought she had a sense of humor or even that theirs aligned.

"According to the supplier of those pipe bombs planted at the Silver Springs houses, the Landsliders are involved—the reason we came into town. You'll be helping us track down their outposts, which means I'm going to brief you on information about the man we're tracking, intel you've got to keep to yourself. Sierra's given us the necessary permissions, because you won't be able to share this with your pack." Navi watched him with an intensity that made his blood burn. As if she was testing him this very moment to see if he'd jump or run the other way.

What she didn't know is he'd been waiting for a chance, waiting for some way to unleash and let his wolf run free for far too long. This sort of fight, against an unknown, powerful enemy—this was something he could throw his whole heart and soul into.

Finn flashed her a grin, his teeth sharpening at the edges. "You had me at danger."

About the Author

Strong women. Strong words.

Katherine McIntyre is a feisty chick with a big attitude despite her short stature. She writes stories featuring snarky women, ragtag crews and men with bad attitudes—high chance for a passionate speech thrown into the mix. As an eternal geek and tomboy who's always stepped to her own beat, she's made it her mission to write stories that represent the broad spectrum of people out there, from different cultures and races to all varieties of men and women. Easily distracted by cats and sugar.

Katherine loves to hear from readers. You can find her contact information, website details and author profile page at http://www.totallybound.com

www.ingramcontent.com/pod-product-compliance
Lightning Source LLC
Chambersburg PA
CBHW050734180626
46814CB00002B/757
* 9 7 8 1 9 1 3 1 8 6 1 3 5 *